"I want yo...

"You're go... ...ur old life," Willow said. "You don't need me there."

"You're wrong. They're my family, but I don't know them. Right now, you're my whole world. I can't remember a time when you weren't in my life. Don't make me do this without you."

"I don't know how to act around rich people. I'll embarrass myself and you in the process."

"I could never be embarrassed by you. And I'm in the same boat. I don't feel like a billionaire. The only constant in my life is you. You're my lifeline."

"And when you get your memories back? What then? I go home and we pretend this never happened?"

"No, I'm not ready to give this, you, up yet. But under the circumstances, we can't promise each other anything either. But go with me. Please."

* * *

Promises from a Playboy by Andrea Laurence is part of the Switched! series.

Dear Reader,

I've waited a long time to find just the right story and hero for my heroine, Willow. I didn't know her name would be Willow. I didn't know she would be a mystery writer. But I knew she had overcome adversity and loss. I knew she was a fighter. I knew she had a sassy husky named Shadow after I lost my own fuzzy boy to cancer in 2019. And I knew she would be the perfect counterbalance to a hero like Finn.

They wouldn't be an ideal match to start, of course. She had a lot of baggage and had worked hard to remove herself from the world and the pain she believed would come with it. He was too wrapped up in frivolity to notice someone like Willow. But by taking away his past, his memories, and his preconceptions about himself and the world, I was able to open his eyes to everything he was missing.

Finn and Willow's book is special to me and I enjoyed writing their story for you. If you enjoyed reading it, tell me! Contact me on my Facebook page or via my website at www.andrealaurence.com.

Enjoy,

Andrea

ANDREA LAURENCE

PROMISES FROM A PLAYBOY

HARLEQUIN
DESIRE

HARLEQUIN®
DESIRE™

Recycling programs for this product may not exist in your area.

ISBN-13: 978-1-335-73509-6

Promises from a Playboy

Harlequin Enterprises ULC
22 Adelaide St. West, 40th Floor
Toronto, Ontario M5H 4E3, Canada
www.Harlequin.com

Printed in U.S.A.

Andrea Laurence is an award-winning contemporary author who has been a lover of books and writing stories since she learned to read. A dedicated West Coast girl transplanted into the Deep South, she's constantly trying to develop a taste for sweet tea and grits while caring for her boyfriend and an old bulldog. You can contact Andrea at her website: www.andrealaurence.com.

Books by Andrea Laurence

Harlequin Desire

Millionaires of Manhattan

What Lies Beneath
More Than He Expected
His Lover's Little Secret
The CEO's Unexpected Child
Little Secrets: Secretly Pregnant
Rags to Riches Baby
One Unforgettable Weekend
The Boyfriend Arrangement

Switched!

From Mistake to Millions
From Riches to Redemption
From Seduction to Secrets

Visit her Author Profile page at Harlequin.com, or andrealaurence.com, for more titles.

You can also find Andrea Laurence on Facebook, along with other Harlequin Desire authors, at www.Facebook.com/harlequindesireauthors!

Prologue

Finn was startled awake by a loud bang and a rumbling that made the plane shudder with turbulence. Normally flying on the corporate jet was smooth sailing, the epitome of luxurious travel, so he instantly knew something was wrong.

His heart was pounding in his chest. He tried to get up out of his seat, but the shaking of the plane knocked him back into the chair. There were five people on board—Finn, the pilot and copilot, a flight attendant and a manufacturing consultant that had joined them at the last minute. The consultant's original flight on a commercial carrier had been canceled and Finn had offered him a ride back to the US from Beijing. As he turned to look at the terrified man in the seat across the aisle from him, he knew the man now regretted taking him up on the offer.

Pushing up and bracing himself on the next seat, Finn fought his way to the front of the plane. He ignored the calls of the buckled-in flight attendant pleading with him to return to his seat.

"What's going on?" he shouted over the chaotic beeping of sensors, the frantic Mayday calls of the pilot and the uncharacteristically loud roar of the engine.

"Mechanical failure," the copilot said as he turned around and looked at Finn with worry lining his brow. "Something has gone wrong with the engine and we're not going to make it to Salt Lake City. We're trying to reroute to Sea-Tac for an emergency landing. You should return to your seat and put on your seat belt, Mr. Steele."

"Screw the seat belt! Put on your parachute," the pilot shouted as he fought to control the steering. "There's one under each seat."

"Parachute?" Finn stumbled and gripped at the door to the cockpit to steady himself. "Are you serious?"

"If we don't make it to Seattle in time, we might have to bail. I'm trying to bring us down to a safer altitude just in case."

Finn swallowed hard. The idea of leaping from the jet into the dark night had never crossed his mind. He was the family wild child, but the risks he took were with women and fast cars. He wasn't the type to jump out of a perfectly good airplane.

The plane jerked hard, sending him stumbling forward. Another shrill alarm sounded from the control panel. Then again, he thought, this was not a perfectly good airplane. He stumbled back to his seat and pulled out the package underneath. The man beside him nervously did the same, slipping the parachute straps over his arms while still securely belted into his leather lounging chair.

Finn put on his own parachute, snapping the clasps over his chest to secure it. His father had insisted that each plane be equipped with parachutes for emergencies. They'd gone over how they worked once when they first bought the planes, but he wasn't sure he'd really listened. He honestly never thought he would need to use it. Who would expect a fancy private jet like this to be anything less than flawlessly maintained?

He groaned and lowered himself into his seat as they rumbled through the air. His father would be incensed if one of the multimillion-dollar corporate jets crashed. And somehow, Finn knew it would be his fault. Everything was always his fault in the end.

Finn was reaching for his seat belt when another loud bang deafened him. The bang coincided with a fireball and the sudden whip of wind through the cabin as the blast created a large hole in the side of the fuselage. Half a heartbeat later, Finn was sucked from his seat and flung into the dark night.

In an instant, there was the sensation of freezing cold with the wind whipping around him. The blackness enveloped him with only pinpoints of light visible in the distance. He couldn't breathe at first. His brain could barely keep up with it all; he was in complete sensory overload.

Finn had no idea how high he was or how far he was from the ground, but he could feel himself start to get light-headed. Gritting his teeth, he pulled the cord and the parachute jerked him to a slower descent. That done, he gave in to the swimming sensation in his head and blacked out.

When he came to, he could see the tops of trees highlighted by the moonlight. He came in hard and fast, blowing through the thin upper branches as he descended into what appeared to be a densely wooded area. Considering they'd been over the Pacific Ocean not long ago, he was ecstatic to find trees underfoot instead of miles of inky black sea.

At least until the sharp twigs and leaves started whipping at him. They cut at his skin like a hundred icy knives. As he descended lower, he tried to cover his face with his arms and he could feel the branches snagging at his clothes.

Then he jerked to a sudden stop.

He looked up and realized the same branches that had attacked him had snagged his parachute.

Now he was dangling from his harness, unsure if he was five, ten or thirty feet from the ground. Finn squirmed, hoping he could untangle the parachute enough to get closer to the forest floor, but there was no getting loose.

Finn considered his options for a minute. He needed to get down from this tree, but there were no tree trunks within his grasp. He couldn't just dangle here until morning and hope someone found him. He could be in the middle of nowhere for all he knew, and he was too exposed up here in the treetops without shelter from the wind. He started to shiver in his thin dress shirt and summer suit coat. Beijing had been a lot warmer in September than wherever he was now. Maybe it was the cold, or maybe it was shock of the accident starting to set in. He couldn't be sure. But he knew what he had to do.

With trembling fingers, he fumbled with the harness. The lower buckle unsnapped easily, but he fought with the second. When it finally gave way, he had no time to react before he slipped out. He fell for what felt like minutes, branches slamming into his ribs and whipping at his arms and legs before he took a thick branch across his forehead and everything went black.

One

Willow Bates was enjoying the brisk morning air on her back deck with a large mug of coffee in her hand. The weather was just starting to cool down in the San Juan Islands community that she called home. Somewhere between Victoria, British Columbia, and Seattle, Washington, the smallest of the islands—Shaw Island—was her blessed retreat. Fall was coming. Unfortunately, that also meant that their stormy season was coming.

And judging by the thick black clouds on the horizon, she wouldn't be enjoying the outdoors for a few days. The weatherman said a severe thunderstorm with high winds was heading their way. That meant she'd likely be cut off from the mainland for a day or two, but she didn't mind. She rarely left her island. There was nothing for her in Seattle but painful memories and traffic.

Her shaggy white-and-gray husky mix traipsed over to her and laid his head on her lap. He looked up at her with his big ice-blue eyes. She scratched him behind his pointed ears and sighed. "We need to get your walk in early today, Shadow. It's going to rain for a few days. I probably need to get out of the house and away from the computer for a while, too."

Shadow lifted his head and replied to her with the grumbling *woo* sound that was common for his breed.

She did need a break. It had been a long week filled with highs and lows, frustrations and break-throughs. As a writer, she had a lot of times like this. It was the creative process. But it could give you a headache staring at the computer for hours on end, lost in another world that was completely under your control and yet totally uncooperative at the same time.

If her older sister, Rain, were here, she would've nudged Willow at some point and thrust a plate of food in front of her. She'd done that all through college as Willow studied and ignored her basic needs. "Coffee is not a food group," Rain always said.

Willow thought of that every time she poured an-other cup instead of fooling with making herself something real to eat. It wasn't as though she didn't eat at all. Her rear end would argue otherwise. But she did live entirely on easy-to-prepare foods she could get in bulk at the warehouse store when she bothered to take the ferry to Victoria or Seattle. She kept a stash of protein bars, enough cans of soup and boxes of crackers to survive a nuclear winter, industrial-size jars of peanut butter and jelly, and an assortment of breakfast cereals that would make any six-year-old proud.

Sure, her sister would argue that they'd grown up as vegans and her diet was seriously lacking in fresh vegetables and fruits. Rain could keep her lecturing for her two-year-old son, Joey, and leave Willow out of it. If cancer hadn't succeeded in killing her, protein bars and coffee surely wouldn't.

She took the last sip of her coffee and set it aside. "You ready to go?" she asked Shadow.

Her dog danced excitedly around the deck and howled at her. He was always ready for a walk.

"Okay, okay. Let me get my jacket."

Willow opened the back door and slipped into the jacket she'd thrown over the kitchen chair. She put her keys, phone and a canister of bear repellent in her coat pockets, then went back outside where Shadow was waiting.

"Are we headed to the beach today?" she asked as they went down the steps of the deck and into the wooded area behind her house.

Shadow's fluffy curled tail disappeared ahead of

her into the trees. He liked to roam free but he didn't go too far. He was too protective of Willow to leave her alone for long. She had gotten him as a puppy not long after she'd moved to the island. She'd finished her last cancer treatment in Seattle a year ago and was keen to get as far away from all of that as she could. Rain had worried about her being alone, so Willow silenced her sister's concerns with the blue-eyed ball of fur.

With a new house and a new puppy, Willow had started her new life here. Shadow had been by her side ever since then. He could read her moods and feelings like a book, forcing her to take a break when she needed one. He wasn't a trained therapy dog, but he had become so much more than just a pet to her.

The woods were very active this morning. The birds in the trees squawked loudly, probably anticipating the weather. She pressed through across the spongy forest floor, stepping over fallen trees and following the makeshift trail she and Shadow had worn into the dirt on their way to the beach.

As she reached the tree line, Shadow greeted her with a loud howl. He'd found something on the beach he was excited about. That could be anything from a fish he'd hauled out of the shallows, the perfect throwing stick or something dead and decaying, which was endlessly fascinating to him for some reason.

"What is it, fuzzy butt?" she asked.

He pranced about and then shot off across the beach toward his prize. She squinted her eyes to try and see if she could spy it in the distance. There was definitely something out there. It was bigger than a fish and not moving. Maybe a seal. They didn't get many of them here, but they did show up from time to time. She walked along the shoreline until the shape became clearer and she realized what she was looking at.

It was a body.

Willow ran across the beach until she got close enough to see it was the figure of a man slumped back over a piece of driftwood. He seemed to be in his thirties or so with golden blond hair and a strong jaw—features that clearly highlighted his handsomeness—but he'd obviously had a bad night. He was beaten and battered with dirty and torn clothing, and there was a large knot on his forehead that had dripped blood down the side of his face.

It was like seeing some angel fallen to earth, cast out of the heavens. His golden curls and perfect skin gave him a cherubic appearance like an old Renaissance painting.

But this man was real. And possibly still alive. There was a bit of color in his cheeks and she could see the faint rising and falling of his chest. She knelt down beside him and reached out to touch his throat. His pulse thumped against her fingertips and she sighed in relief. "Sir?" she asked, but he didn't stir.

Not quite willing to pull her hand away, she reached up to cup his cheek and feel the rough stubble of his beard against her palm. She wasn't inclined to caress strangers—especially ones who looked like they'd been beaten and dumped on a beach by some thugs—but she couldn't stop herself.

When was the last time she'd touched a man? Hugging her two-year-old nephew and brother-in-law, Steve, didn't count. Neither did the poking and prodding from the doctors and nurses at the hospital. Honestly, she didn't really know. Too long.

Shadow sniffed at the man's clothing with enthusiasm, eventually licking the man's face and howling loudly with excitement. That did the trick. The man started at the noise, then winced. Willow jerked her hand away as he groaned loudly and brought a hand up to his bleeding head.

"Damn," he muttered under his breath as his eyes fluttered open.

Willow sat back on her heels and sucked in a ragged breath as the man turned and looked at her. Despite the shape he was in, the man was beautiful, and more so now that he was awake. His large dark brown eyes were fringed with thick lashes any woman would kill for. His gaze ran over her for a moment and a smile curled his full lips, revealing a dimple in one cheek. "Well, hello there, beautiful," he said in the slurred speech of a sleepy drunk. He shifted his weight and groaned again in pain.

"Don't move," she said, ignoring the injured man's flattery and reaching out to press him back to where he was lying. He obviously wasn't in good condition if he thought she was beautiful. She wore no makeup and her hair was a mess under the cap she'd tugged on before she left. "You're hurt pretty badly."

"Don't I know it," he replied with a dry chuckle despite the obvious pain. He looked away from Willow and scanned the beach around him with a frown of confusion lining his forehead. He stopped when he found himself face-to-face with the interested, but patiently waiting, Shadow. The dog was sitting beside him panting heavily, with his pink tongue hanging out of the side of his goofy doggy grin.

"I'm on a beach," he said matter-of-factly.

"Yes, you are."

"With a wolf," he added, as he studied the dog and his large, exposed canines warily.

"Technically he's a wolf dog. Mostly husky, though. He won't bother you unless you mess with me."

"Noted," the man murmured and turned back to look at her. "I'd probably bite any man that messed with you, too."

Willow winced and reached out to examine his head wound. It must be worse than it looked for him to talk like that. "Can you tell me how you got out here?"

He shook his head gently. "I wish I knew. I don't even know where *here* is. What beach am I on?"

"You're on Shaw Island," Willow explained. "Off the coast of Washington State."

"Huh," he said thoughtfully. He wrapped his arm over his ribs and pushed himself up from the sand and rocks until he was sitting upright. "I've never hurt so badly in my whole life. My ribs feel like someone has taken a free shot at me with a baseball bat."

"Is that what happened?" Willow asked. Her island wasn't exactly an epicenter of hard crime. With less than three hundred year-round residents, you couldn't get away with much. The last newsworthy occurrence on the island had involved a rebellious teenager and a joyride in the sheriff deputy's car. But nothing violent that she knew of.

"I have no idea."

Willow frowned. She couldn't understand how a guy could be in this kind of shape but have no clue how he'd gotten that way or where he even was. He must've hit his head pretty hard. "What's your name? Maybe I could call someone for you."

The man opened his mouth to answer and then stopped with a puzzled expression on his face. "I don't know that, either," he admitted.

Maybe he had a concussion. What was she supposed to do for that? Ask questions? "Do you know what day it is?"

"Not a clue."

"Do you know what two times two equals?"

"Four," he answered without hesitation and then shook his head. "I don't get it. I know my alphabet and who the president is. How to tie my shoe… I think. But anything about myself or what happened to me seems just out of my reach."

Willow nodded. "I think we need to get you to a doctor."

A large crack of lightning lit up the sky over the water, followed by a deep rumble of thunder. They also needed to hurry before they got caught in the incoming storm. This beach wasn't accessible by road, so their best shot was to go back to her place.

"Do you think you can stand?" she asked. "My house isn't very far away. If we can get back there, I can call someone to come look at you. We don't have a hospital here or I'd take you there instead."

"I'm not sure, but we can try."

Willow put one of the man's arms over her shoulder and helped slowly hoist him to his feet. He continued to lean heavily on her as they made their way down the beach together. Shadow trotted happily beside them with a piece of driftwood in his mouth.

They had to take their time, but they reached her back deck just as the first few drops of water fell on their heads. Willow unlocked the door and brought him inside, forcing Shadow to leave his prize outside before he could come in.

She helped him to the living room and over to her recliner. The chair had been a lifesaver on long nights when chemotherapy or surgery pains kept her awake and uncomfortable. "Let's put you here," she said.

He lowered gently into the old, squeaky recliner and sighed in contentment. "I think this is the most comfortable chair in the whole world."

"How do you know?" Willow asked, curiously. "You don't even know your own name."

"I *know*," he insisted. "I know a good chair when I sit in one."

Willow shook her head and pulled her phone out of her pocket. "I'm going to call the local doctor and see if he can come by."

"Okay," he said. "I'm not going anywhere."

"Let me just check one last thing…"

The only doctor living on Shaw Island—a retiree who went by Doc—pressed his fingers against his rib cage, and it was like daggers exploding in his chest. He jerked away and made an involuntary screech like an injured animal as tears welled in his eyes.

"Yeah, if they aren't broken, they're at least badly bruised." The older man narrowed his gaze at him and nodded. "Two, probably three of your ribs are cracked is my guess without an X-ray to look at."

He groaned and clutched his abused chest with

his hand. "I could've told you that without the jab-
bing."

"Do they need to be wrapped or something?"

He turned his attention to the woman who'd saved
him as she spoke up. She'd told him her name was
Willow once she returned after calling the doctor.
He didn't think she looked like a Willow. She was
very thin, waif-like in figure, with short, dirty blond
hair and large, dark brown eyes. She was intriguing
to look at, with thick eyelashes and faint freckles
across her cheeks. She just didn't look like a Willow
to him. Then again, he didn't know what he thought
someone named Willow should look like.

"No, it's best to just leave them be," Doc explained. "The muscles of the chest are strong enough
to hold the bones in place until they heal. They're
not at a risk of puncturing his lungs or anything serious. Really, it's a good break to have."

He flinched at the doctor's words. "Are you serious?"

"Well, it won't feel great at first," Doc said with a
small chuckle. "No, you're going to feel like you're
being stabbed every time you try to move for two or
three days. The pain medicine will help, but you'll
do good to just lie still. But then, surprisingly, you'll
wake up one morning and be mostly okay. Just a little sore. Ribs are funny that way."

"I'm not laughing," he quipped.

"Good," Doc said with a serious expression. "It'll

hurt like hell if you do." He turned to Willow. "I thought I might call Ted and see if he had room at his place to take our John Doe in until we can get him transported to the mainland."

As if on cue, a large flash of lightning lit the picture window and the corresponding rumble of thunder shook the walls of the house a moment later.

"He may be stuck here a few days. It's supposed to be a hell of a storm. Early in the season for it, too."

"Don't bother Ted. He has enough going on with Linda sick. I'll keep him here. I have a guest room he can stay in until we can get him to a hospital."

He watched Doc frown at him with concern.

"I don't like the idea of leaving you here alone with a stranger," the doctor said to Willow.

"What's he going to do to me? He can barely lift an arm without crying. I'll be fine. I have Shadow and a shotgun, and if he doesn't have all the sense knocked out of him, he'll stay in bed and behave." Willow turned to look at him. "Are you going to give me any trouble?"

He started to shake his head and winced. Every movement seemed to send a painful shock wave through his whole body. "No, ma'am. I'll be a saint. A very still, very cautious saint."

"See?" She turned back to Doc. "It will be fine. I've faced more dangerous things in my life than John Doe here."

"Okay, but I'll be checking in regularly just in

case." Doc peeled off a prescription from his pad and handed it to Willow. "This is for some pain medication, muscle relaxants and an antibiotic to keep his cuts from getting infected. I put it under your name since he doesn't have one."

She looked up from the pad and seemed to eye him warily. "What about his head? He says he doesn't remember anything."

Doc walked back over to where he was sitting and eyed the lump on his head. It felt like he had an egg trying to break through his forehead. "He took quite a blow to the head. But aside from the amnesia, he seems coherent. I'm no expert on head injuries like this, but I'm confident that once the swelling goes down, he'll remember who he is and how he ended up on our little island. In the meantime, though, you'll need to ice it on and off, and may not want to leave him alone just in case he passes out and falls."

The wind whistled loudly past Willow's home, announcing the storm was getting closer. "I'm going to head on out," Doc announced. "I need to put some plywood over my front windows. You've probably got enough time to run to the general store and get these scrips filled before the worst of the storm comes ashore. An hour at the most."

Willow nodded and walked the doctor out. When she came back into the living room, she eyed him in the chair.

"I'm going to run to the store and get your medications. I won't be gone long. I'm leaving you here with Shadow."

He looked over at the dog. It was deceptively fluffy, hiding big blue eyes and even bigger teeth. It had lain on the hardwood floors and watched him since he arrived. No growling or anything. But the husky watched, and he got the distinct impression that Shadow didn't care for him as much now that he was in his home with his mama.

"Can I go with you?"

She narrowed her eyes at him. "That's probably a bad idea. The road isn't paved on my property and you're going to get jostled around."

"That's okay." He closed his eyes and took a deep breath before forcing himself up out of the chair. "I want to go."

Willow shrugged. "Okay. We'll get some supplies and some clothes for you while Eddie fills these." She held up the prescriptions in her hand before shoving them into a messenger bag and pulling out her keys.

They went outside together where she had a big red pickup truck waiting. It had a step and a handle he used to pull himself up and into the seat. She drove as slowly and carefully as she could on the way to the store, but he felt every divot in the road as they went. He probably should've stayed in the recliner with the wolf dog, but he didn't want to be alone. For some reason, the thought of Willow leaving his sight bothered him. She was his savior, and he was going to stick to her side until he didn't need saving any longer.

To distract himself from the pain, he turned his focus from the road to Willow. He studied the interesting angles and curves of her face as she watched the road…the intricate shell of her ear with the single diamond stud piercing in its lobe… Anything was better than thinking about the pain.

The truck finally met with what seemed like a main, paved highway, to his relief. They'd seemed to be out in the middle of nowhere up until this point. Without the bumps torturing him, he was able to entertain other thoughts—like what a woman like her was doing out here alone. She was young, attractive, self-sufficient, thoughtful…but alone. He was a mystery, but she seemed to be equally confusing.

"You need a name," she said.

"What?" he asked as her words jerked him from his thoughtful trance.

"A name. You don't look much like a John Doe," she said, probably making small talk to distract him during the drive. "But I need to call you something while you're around."

He supposed she was right. He needed a name and John didn't suit him at all. "I guess so. Until I get my memory back, we should pick a name to use. But which one? Most people don't get to choose their names."

Willow made a thoughtful sound as she gripped the steering wheel. "How about… Mark? Allen? Henry? When I was in high school I lived next door to a guy named Jeremy. He was pretty cool."

None of those fit at all. He knew instinctively. But the odds of landing on the right name were slim. They could flip through a baby book, even speak his actual name aloud, and with his head beat to hell, he probably wouldn't know it. "I guess it doesn't really matter. I'll let you pick since I'm in your capable hands. What do you want to call me, darling?"

Her gaze met his for a moment before she turned back to the road with a rosy blush on her cheeks. Apparently men didn't call her "darling" very often. The words had slid from his lips easily, as did the hint of a Southern accent he didn't know he had until that moment.

"Um…since none of those other names seemed to thrill you…what about instead of John, we call you Jack? You look like you could be a Jack."

He didn't hate that. It was simple and easy to remember. "I can live with Jack. Now, all I have to do is remind myself to answer to it."

"Jack it is," she said as she slowed and gingerly turned the truck into a small parking lot. "Now, let's hurry up here so we can get home, give you some pain medicine and get you out of those clothes."

Jack's brow went up suggestively on instinct. "If I wasn't in such rough shape, I'd take you up on that."

Her dark eyes got big as she turned off the truck. "Apparently Jack is a flirt," she said, climbing out.

Jack nodded and took off his own seat belt. He didn't know much about himself, but that seemed to be true enough. At the moment, flirting came easier than breathing. He wished everything else was as simple right now.

Two

Willow left her new patient to wander through the small general store while she headed straight for the pharmacy. There wasn't much trouble he could get into on his own in a place like this. Especially with the store's owner, Mrs. Hudson, watching over everything from her perch at the register.

At the back counter, as always, was Eddie McAlister, Shaw Island's only pharmacist. He was always polite and professional, even helping her with research for her books from time to time when she needed a nontraditional poison to kill off a character or some other medical assistance. As an author, she always wondered if he enjoyed knowing everything about the island residents' private medical matters. Most people, for example, had no idea about Willow's past medical history aside from Doc. It had all happened prior to her moving here. But Eddie knew. He took care of all her hormone replacements. Unless someone handled all their appointments and medical issues off the island or via mail order, Eddie knew.

Small-island life was just like that, she supposed. She'd traded anonymity and privacy for quiet when she moved out here from Seattle.

In her mind, she could easily devise a plot where a small-town pharmacist was murdered to cover up a secret only he was privy to. For a second, she could envision him sprawled out on the floor, papers and pills littering the ground all around him and a knife buried into his chest. *A Prescription for Murder*. Not bad, she thought.

"Afternoon, Willow. Heck of a storm heading this way."

She handed over the prescriptions Doc had written out and shook the disturbing images of Eddie's corpse from her mind. Occupational hazard. "Hey, Eddie. You guys closing up early?"

"Perhaps." He glanced down at the papers curiously and back at her. His weary eyes looked over her with a furrowed brow of concern. "Are you okay?"

"Me? Yes." She realized that the kind of medicine

she was requesting wasn't the norm for her. Or for anyone who hadn't been in a car wreck or washed up on a beach. "Those aren't mine. Doc put them in my name, but they're for a John Doe that washed up on the beach. He's pretty banged up but in this weather, we can't get him to the mainland for a few days."

Eddie eyed the prescriptions and then looked out into the general store at the only other person shopping. Willow followed his glance to the tall, blond man who was studying a Snickers bar as though he'd uncovered the holy grail.

"He's had a bump on the head and doesn't know who he is. Doc took a look at him and thinks he may have cracked a few ribs, too. You can put Jack or John Doe on the label if you need to. I know this isn't exactly a normal situation. I'll pay cash for his medicines. I don't know if he has insurance or not."

He looked like he did. Or if he didn't have it, he just paid cash for any medical expenses because he could. Her shipwrecked visitor didn't exactly look like a homeless drifter. The main character of all her books, Amelia Hayes, would note those details about him immediately. Yes, his suit needed to be burned. It was ripped beyond repair, soaked with seawater and crusted with dirt and blood. There were bits of sand and wood stuck to the fabric here and there, likely from his beach nap. But beneath all that, it was a nice suit. When Jack had gingerly slipped out of the suit coat for Doc's examination, she noticed the tag was for Brioni.

A quick Google search on her phone during his exam had uncovered that the custom-tailored Italian suits started at over six grand and went up from there.

Willow was a successful mystery writer. Amelia's Mysteries did well for her. But she estimated her entire wardrobe, shoes included, had cost less than his jacket alone. Her heroine would have a field day trying to determine who this mysterious man really was. *The Case of the Amicable Amnesiac?* Meh. She'd give that some more thought.

Eddie continued to watch Jack as he wandered through the store like he'd never been in one before. He kept picking up things and studying them before putting them back with a visible wince of pain. "Sure thing," Eddie said at last. "These aren't too expensive without insurance, anyway. It will just take me a few minutes to pull it together."

"Thanks, Eddie. Just give me a shout when it's ready." Willow was eager to return to Jack. She told herself it was because she was worried about him being alone with his head injury. But she also found she just liked being around him. Yes, he was handsome and a bit of a shameless flirt, but she liked his smile and his sense of humor. She wasn't sure what he had been through, exactly, before he showed up in her life, but she wanted to do what she could to help him.

"Washed up on the beach, you say?" Eddie, too, seemed entranced by their unusual visitor. Jack had a commanding presence that demanded it of others, somehow. That or he just stood out like a sore thumb on her boring little island.

"Perhaps. We're not entirely sure. He couldn't have just fallen from the sky."

"Or maybe he did," Eddie said with a conspiratorial wink. "If anyone can figure it out, it's our resident mystery writer. Hey, maybe you can use this in one of your books."

Willow chuckled and turned away from the counter. "You never know," she said as she made her way over to Jack. He was looking at a display of sweatshirts for tourists that said San Juan Islands with a sailboat on the front. There weren't a lot of choices for clothes here, just a few things people might need at the beach or as a souvenir, so he would probably go home with one of those today.

She eyed his broad shoulders and tapered waist. "What size do you think you'll need?"

Jack shrugged. "I don't know."

Willow pulled a sweatshirt from the wall and held it up to him without letting it get defiled by the state of his current clothes. "This looks about right. It's a men's large." She threw the sweatshirt, a T-shirt with a similar imprint, a two-pack of boxer shorts, a pair of jogging shorts and some black sweatpants over her arm. "None of this is very fashionable, but it will have to do for now."

"I'll just be glad to get out of this suit. The wool is starting to get itchy."

"Did you see anything else you wanted? I noticed you looking at the candy earlier."

Jack smiled and shook his head. "I don't need any candy." He bit at his bottom lip for a minute and then laughed. "It's just…and it will sound crazy… but I feel like I've never been in a store like this in my life."

"You mean a little shop like this?"

"No, I mean, like a grocery store. I've walked up and down the aisles looking at dish soap and bags of chips. And while the products themselves seem familiar enough, the surroundings are just completely alien."

"I doubt many people could make it to your age without going into a grocery store. It's probably just the bump on your head. Those memories are locked away with your name and how you got here."

Jack looked at her and nodded, although he seemed unconvinced. "It's bizarre." He reached out for a bottle of soda from the nearby refrigerated case. "I know exactly what this tastes like. I feel like I've had it a hundred times. All these brands are familiar when I see them. I can recall the taste of a Snickers. I know that I prefer them to a Milky Way if given the choice. But other things I should know are just out of my grasp."

"That sounds like it would be very frustrating. Hopefully once the swelling goes down, your memory will return."

"Hopefully."

"You'll also need toiletries," she said and grabbed a nearby shopping basket to carry their purchases. He followed her to the aisle of the shop with soap and other items. "You need it all, so pick out whatever you like."

She watched him look over his choices, selecting a toothbrush and a comb fairly easily. After that, he chose soap, toothpaste and deodorant. "This isn't the right scent, but it will work. How is it I know that I wear Arctic Chill scented deodorant, not Mountain Breeze?"

She shook her head. "Memory is a funny thing. It's why I've never used amnesia in any of my books. It has always seemed an odd thing to me. How can you forget everything, but still remember English? Or how to count? The difference between a cat and a dog? How to walk or even feed yourself? How can you injure yourself in such a way that you can't recall the basic facts of your life and the essence of who you are, but the rest of your knowledge remains? It always seemed like a convenient plot device. Too convenient."

"I assure you this is anything but convenient."

Jack grabbed a small bottle of two-in-one shampoo and conditioner. "This should be enough. I'll be happy to get the sand and stink off of me." As he reached to put the bottle in the basket, he winced and clutched his side.

"I think we're done here. Go sit in the truck and I'll be out in a few minutes. Soon we can get some medicine into you and you can finally clean up and get some rest."

Jack seemed hesitant to leave her with all the things he needed.

"Unless you'd rather pay?" she said with a smile. She knew he didn't have a wallet, ID or any money on him.

"Funny girl," he said. "Keep the receipts. Once I get my memory back, I intend to repay you for this fine sweatshirt and all your other kindness."

Willow put the keys in his hand. "We'll run you a tab. Now go get in the truck."

"You want me to what?"

Jack wished he had a camera to capture the look on Willow's face. For a woman who kept a wolf hybrid as a pet and could handle a shotgun, she seemed downright terrified by what he'd just asked her.

"I wouldn't ask you this under normal circumstances, of course, but I need help."

Willow stood frozen like a deer in the headlights.

But as the truth of his words became evident, he saw her relax a bit. "I suppose you're right."

"Normally when I ask a woman to help me take off my clothes, I buy her dinner first. Or I'd like to think that I would. But I'm afraid I've misplaced my wallet."

Jack stood with his dress shirt and pants unbuttoned, but at that point, he'd run into a snag. He simply couldn't move the way he needed in order to remove his clothing. The pain pills and muscle relaxants were working their way through his system, along with the tomato soup and grilled cheese she'd fed him for dinner, but he needed to get out of these clothes and take a bath. He couldn't wait for the meds to kick in. So he'd asked for her help. He got the feeling he was used to a warmer response from women than he got from Willow.

"Just stand as still as you can," she said as she came around behind him. "I'll do the moving. You be a mannequin."

"Yes, ma'am."

He could feel her warm breath on the back of his neck as she leaned in to peel the shirt from his shoulders. He bit back a wince of pain as she worked the ruined silk shirt down his arms, then breathed a shallow sigh of relief as she tossed it to the floor.

"The pants should be easier," he said.

"Maybe for you," she muttered and gently tugged the trousers down his narrow hips.

He held as still as he could, grasping his ribs protectively. But through the rustle of the fabric, he thought he heard a soft intake of breath. It wasn't him. He was holding his breath to keep from groaning or drawing in the scent of Willow while she was so close. So it had to be her. He looked over his shoulder and noticed her quick assessment of his rear end before casting her gaze to the floor.

He lifted one leg, then the other, to step out of the pants, leaving him in nothing but a pair of fire-engine red Calvin Klein boxer briefs. He looked at his reflection in the bathroom mirror and had to agree with her assessment of his physique. He did have a nice ass. That was good to know. In fact, he had a nice everything. He was in no condition to preen and flex in front of the mirror, but he really wanted to.

Jack had a hard body. He was tan, lean and muscular with broad shoulders and strong arms. His thighs were solid and his calves were hard as rocks. He looked like he took care of himself. Maybe rock climbed or something. The view was only marred by ugly purple-black bruises and bright red abrasions that spread across his skin. He supposed it was weird to admire himself in the mirror, but as far as he was concerned, he'd never seen himself before. Anything could've been hiding beneath that suit.

The thought led him to look at his face at last, and there, he winced again. Not that he was uglier than he expected—far from it—but he was in rough shape. The ache in his head wasn't nearly as bad as it looked, thankfully. But it certainly seemed like the kind of injury that could wipe the Etch A Sketch of his brain clean. He didn't know what he'd hit his forehead on—maybe a ship railing before or while falling overboard—but he'd gone down hard.

"I think I'm probably pretty hot when I haven't lost a fight with a two-by-four."

Willow sat back on her heels and watched him as he admired his own reflection in the mirror. "Careful, Narcissus, or you'll drown looking at yourself."

She was a sassy one, his savior. He liked that about her. She seemed like the kind who could match his mouth when the situation called for it. "Hey, I didn't know what I looked like until now. We've been too busy worrying about other stuff like broken bones and medicine."

"I'm sorry," she said, climbing to her feet. "I should've told you straight away that you were hot. You needed to know that."

He could tell by her flat tone that she was mocking him. He was okay with that, too. "It certainly contributes to my overall morale. So does knowing I'm one pair of underwear away from soaking in a hot bath."

Jack eyed the huge copper soaking tub that was in the corner of her bathroom. It looked divine. And considering that every inch of his body from the hairs on his head to his toenails ached, it was just what he needed. But when he didn't make a move to take off his boxer briefs, he saw Willow stand up abruptly out of the corner of his eye.

"You don't think you can…?" She hesitated. When he looked at her, her cheeks were nearly as red as his underpants.

He wasn't quite sure what to think of his rescuer. She was old enough to have seen a man naked, practical enough to understand why it had to be done, but she seemed very uncomfortable by the prospect. "I can't really bend over, but I'll try. You seem miserable enough as it is."

She audibly sighed in relief. "I'll run the bath. I have some lavender Epsom salts I'll add to it that will help with the aches and pains."

With her back turned and the sound of rushing water filling the room, Jack was able to wiggle out of his shorts and kick them over with the rest of his clothes. They might be salvageable, unlike the suit. He walked over to the fluffy white towel she'd placed on the counter and wrapped it around his waist. He didn't want her to turn around and get an eyeful of what he had to offer—which was also a pleasant addition to his overall package and completely unscathed by the accident.

His interest was piqued by a lovely scent that filled the warm air of the bathroom. "Did you say that was lavender?"

"Yes," she said without turning around.

"It's very nice."

"I like it." Willow shut off the water and tested it with her hand. "It should be ready. Enjoy your bath." She turned, making a beeline for the door.

"Wait. I can't get in there by myself. And Doc said I shouldn't be left alone."

She stopped short with her hand on the doorknob. He didn't hear her curse aloud, but he was pretty certain she'd said some choice words in her head.

"I'm sorry. Really, I am. I take no pleasure in torturing you like this."

"It's not—" she started to argue and stopped short. "It's fine."

"I'm not asking for a sponge bath or anything. If you can just help me get in and out—do it with your eyes closed if you want—that's all I need. I'll shower after this, I promise. But Doc said a bath tonight would be good."

"I know. I heard him. I just wasn't thinking about what that meant." Willow walked reluctantly over to the bathtub and held out her hands. "Come on, let's get you in here."

She braced him as he lifted one leg, then the other, into the tub. "Don't look, Ethel," he quipped, tugging the towel off and putting it aside.

"There's not going to be a way to do this without it hurting, so I say do it quickly."

She was right. Jack took a deep breath and lowered himself into the tub. A bolt of pain shot through his chest, wrestling a groan from his lips and bringing the shimmer of tears to his eyes. He kept his eyelids tightly shut as he reached the bottom of the tub. Stretching his legs out, he sat back and sighed.

"Here." Willow offered a rolled-up towel to put behind his neck.

He accepted the towel and let himself relax into the water. Getting in hadn't been fun, but the scalding hot water felt amazing. Jack closed his eyes and laid his head back. "Thank you," he said.

"It wasn't so bad," she said.

"Not just for this. Thank you for everything. Food, clothes, shelter, medicine… You've been beyond kind to me, and I'm a stranger. You could've just called the cops or the coast guard and got rid of me." A loud rumble of thunder outside made the bathroom windows rattle as he spoke.

"Anyone would've done this under the circumstances," Willow said as she walked to the other side of the bathroom and pulled out her vanity chair to sit at a safe distance. "You have nowhere to go and if this storm is as bad as they say it might be, the coast guard has other things to worry about. I have the room and the time to do it, so I'm happy to."

"You said you were a writer earlier. What do you write? Would I have heard of you?"

Willow's nose wrinkled delicately as she shook her head. "I doubt it, even if you didn't have amnesia. I'm a cozy mystery writer. I've published about thirty books since the start of my career. I've done pretty well for myself, but I'm no household name by any stretch."

"What is a cozy mystery?" he asked. As much as he wanted to just close his eyes and drift away on a cloud of Percocet, he knew he needed to stay focused and conscious until he was out of the tub. She didn't need him drowning in her bathroom. So he would ask her questions to stay awake. Besides, it was easy enough to show an interest in Willow. She seemed like the kind of woman who had a variety of layers. He had the urge to peel a few of them back and see what was underneath. If he felt better, he'd start with the cardigan she'd pulled on.

"It's a subgenre of mystery with an amateur detective that solves crimes. Even though there are murders, they're not too gory and we leave out any details that could be a turnoff for our readers. Think of *Murder, She Wrote*, from back in the eighties. Those were classic cozy murder mysteries."

The name of the show was familiar to him. He could remember watching it with someone as a kid, but he didn't know who. It was incredibly frustrating having this head injury. "I always wondered if that old lady wasn't behind the murders somehow. No matter where she went, someone died."

Willow smiled. "You start to wonder after a few dozen people die, right?"

"So you live out on this little island, just you and your dog, and write books about killing people."

She thought about it for a minute and eventually shrugged. "Basically."

He chuckled for a moment, stopping short when the movement hurt his ribs again. "I'm not sure of much, Willow Bates, but I'm pretty sure you're not like other women I've known."

The light in her brown eyes faded. "No," she said, looking down at the tile floor of her bathroom. "I'm not. I never have been."

Jack's brow furrowed in concern at her response. "I'm not saying that's a bad thing. It's a good thing."

"Is it?" she asked. "Being different hasn't benefited me much over the years. It's actually been pretty lonely."

There was a sadness in Willow's expression as she spoke, and it bothered him. He had plenty of his own troubles at the moment, maybe even more than he knew with his memory failing. But somehow he felt like the best way to repay her kindness was to make her smile. It seemed like an awkward expression on her face when she tried—more like she was baring her teeth to a possible predator. The blank neutrality of her sadness appeared far more comfortable for her, judging by the well-worn frown lines between her eyebrows.

She deserved to smile and really mean it. It lit up her whole face in a way that made her even more

striking in appearance. She already had a pene-
trating gaze, high, prominent cheekbones and full,
pouty lips. Her short pixie haircut just accentuated
her features and heart-shaped face. A genuine smile
would take her from an angst-filled runway model
to a radiant cosmetics model in a glossy magazine.

"It is absolutely a good thing to be different,"
Jack insisted. "Fitting in is boring. There's nothing
special about doing and acting like everyone else.
I don't think I'd be very interested in a woman that
was just a cardboard cutout of what magazines and
television shows said she should be."

That brought a real smile, albeit a small one, to
her face. "My mother used to say that after she made
me, she broke the mold. I would joke that it was because she couldn't handle more than one daughter
like me."

"No, not at all," Jack responded with the sincer-
est expression on his face he could muster. "I'm certain she meant that you're a one-of-a-kind person.
And to the right collector, that makes you priceless."

Three

"There," Willow said with a heavy sigh of relief as she tugged down his new shirt. At last, she wasn't alone in the house with the sexiest naked man she'd ever laid eyes on. It was bad enough that he was hard bodied and not particularly shy. But when he started complimenting her, talking about her like she was some rare gift or something, she didn't know what to think. A man had never said anything like that to her. Of course, Jack also had significant head trauma and narcotics in his system. That was more likely to be the cause of his flattery.

It had taken some more careful maneuvering, but Jack was finally bathed and dressed, and now she could suppress whatever wicked thoughts had crossed her mind during his bath and move on with her evening.

Jack looked down at the brand-new San Juan Islands T-shirt and jogging shorts he was attired in and smiled as widely as if he'd just put on a new designer suit. "They fit."

"They're a little big," she noted. He had broad shoulders, but a thinner, runner's physique, which meant he probably spent a lot of time and money getting his clothes perfectly tailored to fit correctly. "But good enough for you to sleep in. Let's go get you settled into the guest room. I hope it will suit you."

"I don't know if it's the medicine or the bath," he said as he followed her down the hallway. "Maybe both…but I feel like I could lie on a bed of nails and still sleep like a baby tonight."

"That's good. I doubt my guest bed is the greatest bed in the world. It didn't make sense to pay a fortune for something that's never used. In fact, no one has ever slept on it before. You're the first actual visitor I've had since I moved to the island."

Willow opened the door to the smallest bedroom, which she'd set aside for the guests she never had. She supposed she did it out of a sense of expectation her mother had instilled in her as a child. She had lived on a commune with her parents, who shared everything they had. When they divorced and her mom moved to Seattle with her and her sister, she was adamant they had a place with room for guests. It was just the way things were done.

So when Willow looked for a house on the islands, she'd chosen one with three bedrooms. One was the master, one was her office and naturally one should be ready for a guest if she ever had one. She'd lived on this island for over a year now and she'd put sheets on the bed for the first time while he was eating his grilled cheese sandwich.

Who was going to visit her? She hadn't been exaggerating when she said she led a pretty lonely life. Her father had vanished. Her mother and grandmother had both passed away. Her sister had her hands full with her husband and a toddler. Her nephew was too young to visit his aunt without his parents in tow. The Bates sisters didn't have any other family left. At least that Willow knew about. She'd lost touch with most of the friends she'd made in school. Those she did speak to were strictly social media acquaintances, not the kind who would visit your home.

Here on Shaw Island, it was just Willow and Shadow, and had been for a while now.

She went ahead of him into the room and pulled back the fluffy down comforter and sheets. The bedroom decor she'd chosen was as cheerful as she could think to buy. The room had white wood furniture and the comforter was yellow with pale pink roses on it. At the store, it had seemed like the perfect little ray of sunshine for a place that usually had gray skies and rain. Of course, it didn't suit her very masculine guest at all, but he didn't seem to mind.

"Considering I slept on a beach last night with a log for a pillow, this will be great, I'm sure."

He slowly limped past her and lowered himself gingerly onto the bed. Jack eased one leg, then the other, under the blankets and lay back against the pillows with a wince and a groan. "It's wonderful," he said. "The most comfortable bed I ever remember having slept in before."

Willow smirked at his cheeky response. For a guy with no memory, he had a pretty good attitude about the whole thing. She couldn't imagine being so laid-back about the whole situation if it were her. Then again, what could he do about it? Especially when he was trapped on this tiny island in a storm?

She watched him settle in and pull up the blankets with a sigh. "I'm going to go get you a glass of water for your night pills," she said.

She disappeared from the room and went into the kitchen. There, she found Shadow sprawled out across the tile floor, keeping cool while he napped. For him, sixty degrees was warm. And with the house thermostat set at seventy, it was downright stifling for his bristly double coat. He lifted his head to watch her as she stepped over him and got a glass to fill at the refrigerator dispenser. Disinterested, he laid his head back down and returned to his nap.

"Don't get too comfortable," she said. "Once I get our guest settled, you've got to go outside to do your business and I've got to get some writing done. With my latest deadline schedule, I can't afford to lose a whole day of work because some shipwrecked amnesiac derailed my afternoon."

One ice-blue eye watched her as he listened, then he grumbled back at her in the way that only huskies would do. She hadn't deliberately chosen a breed that would talk back, but it did help with the loneliness sometimes. Unless he was being sassy, like now.

"I don't want to hear it. Rain or no rain, you're going out. It's only going to get worse later."

Willow stepped back over her dog and returned to the guest room. There, she found her patient was already asleep. He was sprawled out on his back, propped up by a couple pillows and softly snoring. One arm was draped protectively over his ribs and the other was limp at his side.

She put the glass of water on the nightstand beside the bottles of medication he would have to take in a few more hours. She knew she should turn off the light and leave him to get his rest, but she was drawn in by the rhythmic sound of his breathing. She watched him for a moment as she had that morning on the beach. His face was even more beautiful now with the dirt and blood washed away. His thick golden eyelashes rested on his cheeks, which were rosy once again. If it wasn't for the bandage across his forehead, you wouldn't even know he'd probably just lived through one of the worst experiences of his life. In fact, he looked like she could lean down, kiss him, and he would awaken from whatever evil curse a witch had put on him.

With a sigh, Willow turned off the lamp and left the room. She needed to stop listening to those folklore and fairy-tale podcasts. Her visitor was no secret prince under the spell of a wicked queen. He could be a high-end drug dealer who'd gotten thrown overboard when a deal went wrong on some cartel's yacht. Or a partying playboy who'd drunk too much and fell off his own boat. Either way, nice boys didn't wash up on the beach with amnesia. She'd written enough mystery novels to know that much.

Willow forced Shadow outside for a potty break, standing stoically on the back deck in her raincoat and watching the sky. The rain wasn't falling very hard yet, but she knew it was coming. The inky black of the sky was marred with a swirling gray mass of clouds that would periodically light up with a flash of lightning a few miles offshore. The latest weather reports had the worst of it hitting Shaw Island around two in the morning.

While she waited, she walked along the back of the house, closing and latching the shutters to protect all the windows. By the time she was finished, Shadow was back on the deck, his white paws brown with mud.

She cleaned him up, dried him off and then they both returned to her office to settle in for some late-night writing. She sat down at her desk and turned on her laptop. Shadow curled up on his plush dog pillow and covered his face with his bushy tail to block out the light of the computer so he could sleep.

Willow opened up the file for her latest manuscript. She read over the last few pages she'd written to orient herself and prepared to start where she'd left off. But as her fingers met the keys, she found her heart and her head were not in the mood to write. Not tonight. She had too much real life on her mind for a change.

The mystery of Jack Doe was at the forefront of her thoughts, not who had killed the town's librarian with a letter opener during the Halloween festival. The book would have to wait. She sat back in her chair, frustrated, and stared at the screen without really seeing any of the words.

Who was this man who had crash-landed in her life today? He was handsome and rich, if his clothes were any indication. He could be some Seattle corporate guy who'd fallen overboard at some business affair on the company ship. Or the lover of a rich married woman who'd had to jump into the sea when her husband showed up in his helicopter. No matter what, he didn't belong on Shaw Island, so how else could he have appeared on her beach? A man like Jack hadn't simply fallen from the sky.

Or had he? Eddie had made the suggestion and said that she could figure it out even if no one else could.

Willow frowned and slammed shut her laptop. She was wasting brain cells on this. Chances were his memory would come back at any time and his story would be completely sensible and benign without the slightest hint of high-stakes misconduct or television-like drama. And even if he wasn't some criminal or lowlife hiding from the people wanting to kill him—even if he was just a normal guy who'd had a freak accident—what did it matter to Willow?

Really, honestly, would it change anything about her life in the end?

The truth of the words hit her hard. He might not be an average guy, but she certainly wasn't an average woman, either. She was a hermit, a self-sequestered loner, and for good reason. She hid her hollow shell of a body away from the rest of the world, which might look at her and see she was different. It was easier that way. Easier to avoid the looks and questions of well-meaning strangers. Easier than explaining to people why she didn't get married and start a family with a nice boy like her sister. Easier than looking at people's expressions of pity when they learned the truth about her medical history.

Jack was charming. He had a good sense of humor. He had a dimple in one cheek when he smiled that made her kneecaps turn to butter. And if he hadn't basically landed in her lap, she never would've been exposed to a man like him. A walking, talking temptation like Jack simply didn't show up in a place like Shaw Island, and that made her day-to-day life easier. It made distancing herself and suppressing any kind of emotions or attraction so much simpler.

But now he was here. Lying in the other room. She'd briefly glanced at his naked body when she'd undressed him today and had to turn away as her cheeks flamed with embarrassment and interest. The lure was dangling in front of her, so to speak, making it that much more difficult to be the stoic, chaste loner she'd decided to be.

Even then, there was no point in allowing herself to fantasize that they would ever have more than they had at this exact moment. Jack had a life somewhere. He might not know anything about it, but it was out there. A job, a family, maybe even a girlfriend or a wife. When his memory returned, he would want to go back to all that. And he should. This wasn't where he belonged.

And even if he was interested in her—and she seriously doubted that—it wouldn't last long. Jack was the kind who asked a lot of questions. Tonight, they'd been innocent enough, but eventually he might start wondering about her and why she lived the way she did. It wasn't an easy answer. Or a pleasant one to hear.

When he found out the truth, he would happily

return to his old life and she wouldn't blame him. Whatever it was he'd left behind, it had to be more exciting and glamorous than what she had on this little island. His family and friends would be looking for him, and even if he didn't remember who he was, the news of the missing man would reach them eventually.

So Willow had to be careful not to get too attached to Mr. Jack Doe. He wouldn't be around for long.

Kat Steele paced the kitchen floor, rubbing her very pregnant belly while she walked. Finn was missing. He might even be dead. As complicated as her situation with twins Sawyer and Finn was, losing Finn wouldn't make it any easier. He was her brother-in-law, but he was also the father of her baby. Sawyer would absolutely step up to be the best dad he could be, but she didn't want him to do it because Finn was dead.

She heard her husband, Sawyer, hang up the phone and come into the kitchen. She stopped and looked at him, desperate for some news. "Have they found him?"

"They found the plane," Sawyer said with a somber expression on his face.

She knew this couldn't be easy on him. Possibly losing his brother was bad enough, but Finn was his identical twin. That had to be like losing part of himself, somehow. "And?"

"It crashed in the woods in the middle of nowhere in Washington near the Oregon border. No one else was injured, but they found four bodies in the wreckage."

"How many people were supposed to be on the jet?"

Sawyer didn't meet her gaze for a moment. "Four. Two pilots, a flight attendant and Finn. All four bodies were burned beyond recognition, so they can't positively identify any of them yet."

Kat groaned and lowered herself onto a nearby barstool. "So we won't know for sure until they look at the dental records, right?" She was grasping at hope for the sake of her husband and daughter. But she knew it wasn't likely to end well for them.

"Yes. They're transporting all the bodies back here once the crash site has been released by the FAA. Then we'll know for certain."

Kat closed her eyes and bit back tears. Finn had been a massive pain in the ass nearly from birth. She'd almost married him, in some mistaken drive to build a proper family. But he had been working hard at becoming a better person lately for his daughter's sake. He didn't deserve to die like this. No one did.

She felt Sawyer's arms wrap around her and she gave in to the embrace. When he held her, it felt like the world couldn't get to her or her daughter.

But even Sawyer's strong arms couldn't protect her from this grief. It only added fuel to it, knowing how much he must be hurting, too. How much the whole family must be grieving his loss...

"I want to say something, but I'm not sure how to do it. I can't say it to anyone but you. They'd think I was crazy, but I hope that you'll have an open mind."

Kat sat up and wiped the tears from her cheek. Sawyer was the serious twin, a man of few words, so if he had something to say, she would let him, even if it were crazy. "Tell me."

He glanced over her shoulder at the wall as he tried to figure out the words. "I don't want to upset you or get your hopes up. But I just... I feel like if Finn were dead, I would know it."

"What do you mean?"

Sawyer shook his head. "It's not like I'm saying we had some psychic twin connection or anything like some twins claim. We didn't. We've been opposites from the start. Mirror images of each other. But he doesn't feel dead. I feel like I would know if he were really gone."

Kat frowned. Sawyer had lived a life of privilege, never having to face real loss before. "Losing someone never feels the way you expect it to. When my parents were killed in an accident, it seemed like they were just on a trip and would be home anytime. Even after I identified their bodies, I kept waiting for a call or something from them. When it happens so suddenly, it feels harder to process. At least it was for me."

"I know what you're trying to say. And yes, when they identify him for certain, I'll give up the ghost. But I would be able to feel it if he were dead. I've had a headache since yesterday before the phone call. No medicine will touch it. I think Finn is hurt. Maybe he hit his head. But I believe he's alive."

Kat wasn't quite sure how to be supportive of her husband in the face of his denial. They'd found four bodies. Finn was more than likely amongst them. She hated it for him and his family. She hated it for her daughter, who would never get to meet the funny, carefree man who'd helped to make her. But hating reality didn't change it.

"You don't believe me." Sawyer's face was red with indignation. "I shared something very personal with you and you don't believe me."

Kat sighed. "I don't know, honey. I want to believe you. I want more than anything for Finn to be okay. Maybe he is and you're right." She reached out and stroked his arm. "We will know for sure, soon."

Jack expected to be awoken by the alarm reminding him to take more medication. Instead, he was roused from his sleep by a brilliant bolt of lightning hitting too close to them for comfort. The whole house immediately shook with the thunder, jerking him upright in bed. Thankfully, the rumble smothered his shout of pain as his rib cage protested the sudden and unanticipated movement.

Clutching his ribs, he lowered back against the pillows with a groan. He reached out for the lamp, hoping it would illuminate the clock and prove it was almost time for him to take his medicine. But the click of the knob yielded no results. The room remained dark. The clock face was dark. The house was silent, no hum of the heat or appliances in another room. He realized then that the storm must've knocked the power out.

The creak of the door opening sounded unusually loud in the quiet house. When he looked over, he saw the illuminated face of Willow with a flashlight in her hand. The bright bulb highlighted the interesting angles of her face as her dark eyes searched the room for him. "Are you okay?" she asked.

"Yeah, I just got startled. Hurt like hell, but I'll live."

As if in response, the skies seemed to open up overhead, and the lightning and thunder was joined by the roar of hard rain coming down on the roof and windows. "The power is out," she said. "It will be until tomorrow, at the earliest. We don't exactly have an emergency power crew on standby here. They're all stuck on the mainland in storms like this. I have a generator that will kick in and keep the refrigerator and a few appliances running, but that's about it."

Jack sat up and swung his legs out of the bed as

gingerly as he could. "Do we need to do something? Cover the windows?"

"I did all that after you went to sleep. We may want to move into the living room, though. Without the heat running, this place is going to get chilly pretty quickly. You'll be more comfortable by the fireplace."

"Okay." Jack pushed up from the bed and Willow handed him the flashlight.

"If you can take this, I'll get your stuff and bring it out."

He watched her gather his blanket and his medicine and follow him into the hallway and to the living room. The room had vaulted ceilings with heavy wooden beams and a stone fireplace against one wall that went all the way to the top. She put his blanket on the recliner and set his water and pill bottles on the small table beside it.

"Go ahead and get comfortable. I'll get a fire going."

Jack watched with curiosity and a little guilt as Willow moved quickly to light a fire. He noted how carefully she stacked the logs, placing smaller pieces between them along with tiny chunks of what looked almost like sawdust cakes. She was experienced enough that it caught quickly and within a few minutes, the fire was on its way to becoming a large and warm light source for them both.

He turned off the flashlight and placed it on the table beside him. "You must lose power here a lot."

"More than I'd like," she admitted. "But I keep a fire going in here most of the winter anyway. This close to the ocean there's not a lot of snow or ice, but the wind is awful and the cold just goes straight through to your bones."

Jack caught movement out of the corner of his eye and noticed her large dog joining them. He sought out his oversize fluffy pillow by the fireplace and settled onto it. Resting his head on his paws, he watched Jack in a way that made him uneasy. Like the dog didn't trust him with his mama. Jack smothered a smile. His mama could take care of herself. Jack was the one at her mercy.

The rain started coming down harder, filling the room with a loud roar as the wind whipped it into sheets that pummeled the house. Thunder continued to rumble around them with the occasional nearby flash of lightning dancing over the living room skylight that faced the woods. Combined with the hum of the generator that had finally kicked in, Jack was fairly certain he wouldn't be falling asleep again anytime soon.

"Would you like some hot tea or something?" Willow asked. She was standing with the fireplace behind her. The flames had grown enough that the light shone through the fabric of her thin cotton pajama gown. He could easily make out the narrow outline of her hips and the slight cut in of her waist before it widened to her chest. She didn't have a very voluptuous figure, but it was womanly enough and he found himself being tantalized by the unexpected glimpse of it he was being given. The nightgown itself was fairly short, falling midthigh and providing him with a full view of her long, feminine legs and dainty feet with pink toenail polish.

It was a silly detail to notice, but one that made him smile. His savior might seem like a hard wilderness woman on the outside, but there was a soft, unexpectedly feminine side to her that had his full attention, as well.

"Jack?"

His gaze shifted quickly to her face. "Yes?"

"Would you like some herbal tea?"

"Yes, please," he said with a smile he hoped would cover up the fact that he'd been admiring her figure.

"Okay," she said with a curious wrinkling of her brow. "I'll go make it."

Jack leaned back into the recliner with a sigh as she left the room and followed it with a groan as he once again moved too quickly. He welcomed that pain this time, though. The sharp sensation would hopefully dull the arousal that had warmed his bloodstream faster than the fire had. Even with no memory of his past, he now knew for sure that women played a very large and important role in his life.

He was also certain that things with Willow had suddenly become decidedly more interesting.

Four

As comfortable as her recliner was, Jack found himself moving over to the couch, where he could sit beside Willow and share his blanket with her. It wasn't an entirely magnanimous gesture; he wanted to be closer to her, but if he could help her stay warm, all the better. She had pulled a chenille robe on over her nightie when she returned from the kitchen, which disappointed him a bit, but he imagined it wasn't the warmest outfit under the circumstances. She settled in on the other end of the couch and happily tugged her end of the blanket over her bare legs to chase away the chill.

He took a sip of the tea she'd made for him. It had

a floral taste with a sweetness he didn't recognize, which wasn't surprising given the situation. "What kind of tea is this?" he asked.

"Chamomile with local honey. It's good for relaxation and sleep, plus it helps with my allergies. I drink it nearly every night. Sometimes I get a little spun up writing and a cup of this helps me turn off my brain and get some rest."

"It's good." He took another sip and looked around the room for what they could discuss next. "So since we're awake with nothing to do, tell me more about you, Willow. I know you're a writer and you live on this island with your dog. What else is there to know about you?"

Her eyes widened for a moment at his question. "There's not much to know. Honestly, I'm not that great talking about myself. I'm better at making things up."

There was plenty to discuss—of that he was certain—but he just had to convince her to open up. "Well, I can't talk about myself. We can't discuss movies or literature. So unless we're going to stare awkwardly at each other all night, how about you start at the beginning."

Willow let a blast of air out of her lungs in resignation. "Okay. Well, I grew up not far from here in a commune on the mainland. My parents were major hippies and vegans before it was really a thing. My dad was one of the farmers that grew food and supplies, and my mother worked taking care of the children in the community. It was a different kind of upbringing. We had electricity, but we didn't have televisions or video games. There was one landline phone everyone shared. We played outside and with the other children. I read every book we had in our little library. My sister and I were basically free to roam because it was a safe place for us. I really loved my life there.

"Then my parents split up," she continued. "My mom decided she didn't want to stay with my father there, so she packed us girls up and we moved to Seattle to live with my maternal grandmother."

"How old were you when you left?"

"I was about eleven, I think. My sister was thirteen."

Jack wasn't sure what his childhood was like, but if he had to guess, it wasn't anything like hers. "I bet that was a shocking transition."

"It was devastating. Public schools, buses, traffic, pollution, fast food, violence, sitcoms…things that were normal to other people were completely alien to us. There were good things, but they were outnumbered by the bad for me. I remember crying and begging Mama to take us back home. She may have even considered it. But then my grandmother got sick and we had to stay and take care of her. We never did go back."

Jack could tell that she didn't like talking about

herself, so he was pleased she was indulging him even if he did have to prompt her for details. "Did you opt for college or jump right in to writing?"

"I got an English degree," she said. Willow perked up a bit as though shifting to her writing was far more comfortable a discussion. "I wasn't quite sure what I wanted to do and it seemed like a good way to avoid facing real life for a few more years. I found I really enjoyed my creative writing classes and my professor encouraged me to pursue fiction writing, so I tried my hand at it. It was something I could do while helping out my mom at home when she got sick. By the time she passed away, I had already published a couple mysteries and I was doing well enough to be able to live on my own."

It seemed even discussing her writing wasn't safe. He noticed the sadness in her eyes despite talking of her success. He could tell the cloud of losing her mother hung over it, tainting it. "It sounds like you lost a lot of people in your life at a young age."

Willow nodded. "Cancer is a bitch," she said with a tone of finality that ended that line of discussion.

"When did you decide to move here?" he asked.

"There were a few years where I thought Seattle was where I would stay. I needed to be close to civilization for a while," Willow said with a pained expression pinching her face. "But when I was able to get away, I came here. It reminded me of where I grew up, wild and yet safe at the same time."

"Don't you get lonely out here all by yourself?"

She narrowed her gaze at him. He watched a confusing mix of emotions dance across her face for a moment before she shook her head. "I prefer to be alone. It makes it easier to work without distractions."

"Yeah, I can see that. But don't you want to have a family one day? At least a partner to share your life with? You can't meet someone if you never leave your house."

He watched Willow stiffen slightly before reaching out to set her mug on the table. "No, I don't want any of that. I knew early on that the normal life path wasn't for me. My older sister, Rain, did the husband-and-kid thing. I can always visit her if the urge to cuddle my nephew strikes, but that's a choice I made. There are just certain things about my family that don't need to be passed along to another generation. Motherhood is not in the cards. I don't think love is, either. And I'm okay with that. I have my house, my community. I have Shadow, of course. And dogs are superior to people in so many ways."

She chuckled softly at her observation, but the laughter didn't reach her eyes. There was something sad there instead. The way she looked at him as she spoke told Jack that she was lying to him about how she felt. Perhaps even lying to herself. She didn't want to be alone, not really. She was just…scared… perhaps to be with someone. Perhaps she'd lost too many people in her life to risk having it happen again. Maybe she'd been hurt in a past relationship. He could understand wanting to swear off love if she'd been burned. But not everyone was a bad guy. Not everyone would leave her. Jack, for example, wasn't a bad guy. At least he didn't think so.

It was the way she looked at him then that urged him to lean closer to her. When she didn't pull away, he knew he was reading her right. He reached out to cup her cheek and draw her lips up to his own.

It started off as a soft, hesitant kiss. With no memories of his past, Jack felt like some awkward kid kissing his first girl under the bleachers after school. But it all came back to him pretty quickly. He deepened the kiss, holding her face in his hands, drawing her closer and drinking her in. She tasted like the honey from her tea, and the sweetness caused him to groan against her lips.

Willow reached out and wrapped her warm palm over his knee. Even through the wool blanket, her touch was enough to make his insides turn molten with a familiar need that wore away at his self-control. He wanted to touch her. Explore more of her body and reacquaint himself with the female form. He slipped his hand from her cheek to her shoulder and then lower.

Jack knew the instant he'd pushed her too far. Willow froze in place, her lips suddenly hard and unyielding when they had been soft a moment before. Half a second later, she was on the far side of the couch and he was aware of the chilly absence of her body close to his. Not even the fireplace could take the place of her warmth.

"I—I'm sorry," he said instinctively, although he wasn't entirely sure what he'd done wrong. Reaching out to touch her had felt like the most natural thing in the world to do. But he'd been incorrect in his instincts where Willow was concerned. He had barely grazed her chest. He hadn't even gotten far enough to feel the weight of her breast in his hand before she was gone. Maybe he'd moved too fast with someone he hardly knew. Maybe she'd had second thoughts about making out with her strange visitor with an unknown past. She was right to hold back. He could be anyone, anything. He couldn't find any prison tattoos, but maybe he was afraid of needles. He didn't think he was a bad person, but how many good people wash up on a beach in his condition?

"It's not your fault." Willow tugged her robe closed with her fists, effectively closing off her body from him. "I just… I never should've kissed you. That was stupid of me. I led you on and I shouldn't have. You're in no condition for…"

"I'm feeling better every minute."

She wrinkled her nose. "That's the medication, not the curative powers of my kisses. There are other reasons. It's a bad idea all around." Willow got up from the couch and went to stoke the fire with the iron poker leaning against the stone hearth.

Jack reached out for her, but the low grumble of a growl stopped him short before he could grasp her wrist. He looked to see that her dog was no longer asleep on his pillow but had moved between the two of them and was watching Jack warily. He drew back his hand and the growling stopped.

"It's okay, Shadow bear," she said, reaching out to stroke the dog's head. "He's very protective of me."

"I can see that."

He leaned back onto the couch, letting Willow escape and soothing the concerns of her furry guardian. There was no sense in pushing her. Like it or not, he was stuck with her on this island until the storm blew through and the ferry was running again. There was no reason to make things more awkward with his host than they already were.

But what he did know, deep down, was that he'd never kissed a woman like Willow before. And he liked it. Very much.

"What are you doing?"

Sawyer looked up from his suitcase with a guilty but determined look on his face. Kat wouldn't be happy with him, but he had no choice. "I'm packing to fly to Seattle."

Kat sighed and sunk down onto the bed beside his luggage. "Just because Finn's body wasn't one of the four they recovered doesn't mean he's alive, honey. That hole that blew into the side could've sucked him out over the ocean or the woods well before the crash and we'll never find him."

Sawyer continued to pack. "That's what they told me. It's very logical, of course. But I've got to go. I've got to at least look for him. It might be a lost cause, but he's my twin brother. He'd do the same for me."

"Would he?"

Sawyer paused and looked at his wife. The beautiful redhead had been the center of his universe since she marched into his sister's wedding reception and slapped him hard across the face. Now, in her third trimester of her pregnancy, she was practically glowing with radiant beauty. But he wouldn't let her talk him out of this.

With a heavy sigh, he tossed his toiletry bag into his suitcase and flipped the lid closed. "My brother is a complicated person to love. There are times when I've resented the hell out of him. Times when I felt like he practically got away with murder, living his life without consequences while the rest of us cleaned up his messes. He's a hedonistic playboy. Absolutely. But deep down, my brother is a good person. And yes, I do think he would look for me. He might seduce my nurse while sitting by my bedside while I was in a coma, but he'd be there. So I have to go."

Kat nodded in resignation. "How long do you think you'll be gone?"

"A couple of days at the most. I really don't know what I'm going to do once I get there. Talk to the local police. The coast guard, maybe. Visit a few hospitals and see if they have any John Does I could try to identify. But I know I'm tilting at a windmill."

Kat pushed herself up from the bed, belly first, and wrapped her arms around him. Sawyer buried his face in her auburn hair and inhaled the scent of the shampoo she used. He needed to breathe in enough of her to last him until he got home.

"If you need anything while I'm gone, call Mother or the girls. I know Morgan or Jade would be here in a flash. Actually, what about staying with one of them while I'm gone?"

"I'm pregnant, not an invalid. I'll be fine alone. I lived alone a long time before the Steele family crashed into my life."

"Yes, well," he said in a begrudging tone, "don't be surprised if they drop in to check up on you."

"You told your sisters that you're leaving?"

"Yes," he admitted.

"*Before* you told me?" Kat asked with an irritated arch in her eyebrow.

He had to tread carefully here with his hormonally charged wife. "Morgan and Jade were both there this afternoon when we got the news about the dental record results. We discussed me going out there. Otherwise, of course I would've told you first. You're my wife. The mother of my future child. You're my world. That will never change."

Kat dropped her forehead against his chest as her annoyance faded away. "Hurry home to me, Sawyer Steele. My baby has probably already lost one father. I need the other one."

Willow looked at herself in the bathroom mirror and frowned. She felt stupid. It had been two days since the kiss and she'd been dancing around Jack as though he were going to jump her bones at any moment. Ridiculous. He hadn't so much as looked at her suggestively since the night of the storm. He'd been a perfect gentleman and guest.

Initially, he slept a lot. And as his pain and the associated medications decreased, he was even helpful around the house. He'd attempted to cook a few times and tidied up the best he could. He'd helped her clean up outside after the storm, too. He couldn't haul broken branches or climb up on the roof to throw a tarp over an area that had lost shingles, but he did what he could to be a help and not a hindrance while Willow did those things.

But he hadn't laid a hand on her. Jack probably thought she was scared of him, and she felt bad about that. Honestly, he hadn't done anything wrong. When Jack had kissed her, she'd panicked. It wasn't because she didn't want to kiss him. She did. So badly. It was just that she hadn't kissed a man since her treatments and surgery.

In the moment, it was all too much. Before that night, she hadn't given any thought to how she'd react in that situation because part of coming to this island was to make sure she was never put in that kind of scenario. Living alone, writing her books, isolating herself on this island…it was all by design. She wanted to put that chapter of her life, and everything that came with it, behind her.

She'd lived the past fifteen years of her life knowing that one day, she would likely develop breast cancer. Her grandmother and mother had both succumbed to it within a few years of each other. They'd had the gene that predisposed them to breast and ovarian cancer, and with her family history it was almost a certainty. And after years of screening, a questionable spot had finally shown up on her mammogram. Willow knew the instant she saw it that it would be cancer. And she was right. The doctor had been optimistic since they caught it so early. Perhaps only a lumpectomy and some chemotherapy would be required.

Willow was not so optimistic. She'd watched her mother slowly wither away as she tried all kinds of holistic remedies. Mother insisted the mainstream treatment was worse than the disease, and in a way she was right. But by the time she finally agreed to the chemotherapy, there was no real point.

Willow had firsthand experience with what this cancer could do. So when the doctors delivered the bad news, she had already decided what her path forward would be. It was drastic. Her doctors seemed surprised that she wanted to take it that far. But she couldn't be dissuaded. A full mastectomy and a full hysterectomy was the only way to be certain. If she survived the breast cancer, the BRCA gene still left her vulnerable to relapse and ovarian cancer, as well. So she had them take it all. If she didn't have any of those parts, they couldn't try to kill her later.

Rain told her she was acting out of fear not logic, but Willow didn't want to tiptoe around this. She would use a sledgehammer on the thumbtack of her cancer. And it was just as well. As she'd alluded to Jack, Willow had no interest in passing this curse on to another generation anyway.

The doctors thought she might regret her decision. Her sister certainly disagreed. She was very vocal about it. But Willow had made up her mind and it was her body. And after the painful surgeries, a long recovery and chemotherapy, she didn't ever want to see the inside of another hospital again if she could avoid it.

And she hadn't regretted it. Until now.

Turning around, Willow started the shower to let the water warm up. Then she pulled off her shirt, padded mastectomy bra and pajama pants. Looking down at the mangled remains of her chest, she knew exactly why she had panicked that night on the couch. She had opted out of the reconstruction surgery. She couldn't bear going through more procedures and more pain just so she could fit the image of what a woman should be. Where her breasts once were, now was only flat, rippled skin with a pair of scars that were still pink and healing.

No one had touched her chest since the surgery. But Jack had come very close. When she was alone, she didn't bother with the mastectomy bra that gave her the illusion of a slight figure. After Jack's arrival, she'd put one on, but she hadn't worn it to bed that night.

What would've happened if she'd let him touch her? If he'd realized she was a shell of the woman she'd once been? There were no nipples to harden and press against his eager hands. No full globes for him to caress. She couldn't bear to see the desire in Jack's eyes die away when he realized the truth. Willow would rather run and have control over the situation than be rejected.

But as his lips had touched hers and he'd moaned with desire, it had felt so amazing. It was nice to be wanted as a woman again. Even for just a moment, until she ruined it all.

When she came into the living room after showering, Jack was propped up in the recliner. He had made himself a bowl of cereal and brewed a pot of coffee for them both.

"Good morning," she said, as she went into the kitchen and poured herself a cup.

"Good morning," he responded. "You have an amazing cereal collection."

She chuckled as she added cream and sugar to her cup. "My sister wouldn't agree. She says I don't eat real food."

"Well, these Lucky Charms are great. Oh," he said, setting aside his bowl, "your cell phone was ringing while you were in the shower."

"Thank you." Willow walked through the living room to where she'd left her phone on the charger. The missed-call banner on the screen said that Doc had called. She hit the button to call him back and he picked up a moment later.

"Good morning, Willow. How is our patient doing?"

She glanced over her shoulder at the man in her easy chair. "Jack's getting around better."

"Jack? Has his memory returned?"

"No. He still has no idea who he is. But we had to call him something."

"Ah, that's a shame. I was hoping for a miraculous recovery. Did you two fare okay with the storm? The power was out for a long while this time."

"It was fine. I had a fire going and the generator kept the food from spoiling."

"I'm glad. I'm sorry I didn't call sooner, but I had a tree land on our carport and I've been dealing with that. I figured if there was an issue, you'd call. But today I have some good news. The ferry to Seattle is up and running again. I called over to a friend of mine at Harborview Medical Center. They're expecting Jack later this afternoon. With any luck, they'll be able to track down who he really is and he'll be out of your hair before too long."

Willow didn't respond. She didn't know what to say. She hadn't been expecting this call so soon. Of course she wanted Jack to get the help he needed. But at the same time, there was a part of her that wasn't quite ready to let him go yet, either.

"Willow?"

"Thanks, Doc," she said. "I'll let him know." Willow hung up the phone and took a sip of her coffee. "Good news."

With a groan, Jack pushed up from his chair and carried his bowl into the kitchen. "What's that?"

"Our connection to the mainland is restored. We can finally get you to a real doctor in Seattle where they can take X-rays and treat you properly."

"Oh, okay," he said, although he didn't sound very excited. She tried not to think too much about why.

"Maybe they'll even be able to check the missing-person reports to see if someone is looking for you. I'm sure your family is worried."

"If I have one," Jack said.

She was certain he had one. A man in a designer

suit with an expensive watch didn't go missing without anyone noticing. Even if he didn't have family, he had friends, employees or a lover who would know he was gone. Maybe that was why she was hesitant to take him to Seattle. The knowledge that he probably wouldn't come back.

"I can check the ferry schedule and drive you down there when you're ready."

Jack turned to Willow and frowned. "Wait. You're not going with me?"

She knew it probably sounded horrible, that she would just drop a man with brain damage on a boat and wave goodbye. But she couldn't go back there. Harborview was where she'd had her surgeries and treatments. She just couldn't. Just thinking about the scent of the disinfectant and the long stretches of linoleum-lined hallways made her chest tighten with anxiety.

"You'll be fine. I'll give you some cash to get a cab from the ferry terminal to the hospital."

"It's not a question of how I get to the hospital," Jack said. "I mean, what happens when I finish my exam and all the tests? What if no one is looking for me? Where do I go? I know I don't have any right to ask anything of you, but I don't want to go alone. I know I'm just some stranger that's been sleeping in your guest room for a few days, but you're basically the only person in the whole world that I know.

You're my only and best friend right now. I'd really like you to go with me."

Of course, he'd managed to make her feel terrible for not going. "I don't like hospitals, Jack."

He approached her and cupped her upper arms with his warm hands. "Please, Willow," he pleaded. His large brown eyes were like a big, sad puppy dog, wearing away at her resistance. "I'll find a way to make it up to you, I promise."

She shook her head, knowing that it was a lost cause. She was going back to the hospital. At least this time they wouldn't be sticking *her* with the needles.

Five

Jack stepped through the doors from the MRI wing of Harborview Medical Center and found Willow waiting for him there. It had been a long day of tests and exams, but thankfully this was the last one. The nurse had told them he could go for the day, but to stay in town. They would reach out to him tomorrow with the results and he might need to come back for more tests.

Willow was curled in a ball in the corner of the waiting room. Her knees were drawn up to her chest with her large cardigan wrapped around her. Her head was resting against the wall with her eyes closed. She looked so small and fragile sitting there. As though she were the patient instead of him.

He felt guilty. She told him she didn't like hospitals and he'd asked her to come with him anyway. It had apparently been a stressful day for her just being here. He supposed that after losing several members of her family to illness, a place like this probably held a lot of bad memories for her.

It made him wish he could treat her to a night out. A nice dinner and a stay at a fancy Seattle hotel. It seemed like the right thing to do. If he had a penny to his name. A lot of things about his life had felt weird since he'd woken up without his memory, but not having any funds at his disposal bothered him more than most.

"Hey," Willow muttered as she sat up and sleepily rubbed her eyes. "How did the MRI go?"

"Fine. I found out I'm not claustrophobic, so that's good to know." He grinned at her, trying to lighten the mood. "I'm all done for the day."

Willow looked down at her watch and frowned. "The last ferry to the island left an hour ago, so it looks like we're staying here tonight."

"It's for the best," he said. "The doctors said I might need to come back in the morning if the test results find something that concerns them."

She nodded. "I should've thought of that before we left and brought an overnight bag for us. As it is, we'll have to find a pharmacy where we can get some essentials for the night. Hopefully we can find something nearby."

Jack walked over to where she was sitting and held out his hand to help her up. "I'm sorry today ran long. I promise you that once I have things straightened out, I will pay you back for everything. Not just the hotel, I mean. But food, clothes, medicine, your time... I know I've been an inconvenience from the moment you found me."

Willow looked down at his hand touching hers and gently untangled her fingers from his own. "It's not a problem, Jack, really. I have plenty of money. I have the time. To be honest, your arrival is the most exciting thing to happen in my life in a long time. If it wasn't for the fact that you were hurt, I'd enjoy the change to my routine. Life will surely be boring without you."

There was a sadness in her eyes when she spoke that Jack hadn't noticed before. It did feel like their time together was coming to a close. He couldn't hide out on her island forever. Eventually he would get his memory back or someone would come looking for him. Part of him wished it weren't true. Like somehow things would be easier if he could start fresh with Willow and never look back.

"Okay. Let's go find a hotel," she said. "And then we'll get something to eat. I'm sure you're looking forward to something other than soup and breakfast cereal."

"I don't have a single complaint," Jack replied with a grin.

They headed down the hallway together to the exit of the hospital. As they were reaching the lobby, they passed a woman in a wheelchair. Jack didn't pay much attention to the patient, but a few steps later, he realized that he was walking alone. Turning around, he saw Willow frozen in her tracks. Her wide eyes were locked on the woman in the wheelchair, her lips trembling but wordless.

Jack turned to the woman in the wheelchair to see what he was missing. This woman was likely a cancer patient at the hospital. The thin remains of her hair were wrapped in a bright pink handkerchief. Her face was thin and sunken in with dark circles beneath her eyes. She was the embodiment of frail with arms that looked like a rough nurse could snap them putting in a new IV. Her eyes were shining gems, the spirit still alive despite the ravages of the illness that had brought her here.

He looked back at Willow and the pieces finally clicked into place. This woman had cancer. Being in the hospital was bad enough, but seeing her like that no doubt reminded Willow of losing her mother and grandmother to it. He didn't know how long ago they'd passed away, but judging by the look on Willow's face—large, fearful eyes, tense jaw and firmly pressed lips—it wasn't long enough. She actually looked like she was riding along the edge of panic.

As if on cue, Willow drew in a ragged breath and started frantically wheezing. The woman in the wheelchair watched in alarm as Willow clutched her chest and backed up hard against the far wall to brace herself.

"Willow?" Jack asked, unsure. "What can I do?" He knew better than to ask what was wrong when she could barely breathe and waste the words.

"Leave," she managed between gasps.

Jack didn't hesitate to wrap his arm around her and guide her to the front exit. Outside, he led her to a concrete bench and sat her down. The sun was just setting and the cool air was a refreshing shock to him after so many hours in the hospital. He hoped it was the same for her. Some nice fresh air without the scent of disinfectant and death tainting it.

Willow dropped down to the bench and buried her face in her hands. After a few moments, her shoulders were shaking with raw tears instead of the desperate breaths of her earlier hyperventilating.

The whole situation was unexpected for Jack. Since he'd woken up on the beach, Willow had been his rock. Strong. Independent. Seeing her break down like this was unsettling. Unsure of what else to do, Jack sat on the bench beside her and wrapped a comforting arm around her shoulders.

"I shouldn't have asked you to come," he said after a few minutes of silence. "You told me you didn't like hospitals, but I was being selfish, not wanting to come here alone. I'm sorry, Willow."

She shook her head, wiping the tears away with

the back of her hand. "No. You couldn't have known. Even I wasn't sure how it would be. I got cocky after going all day without more than a twinge of anxiety. And then I saw her and everything hit me all at once."

"I imagine it brings back a lot of bad memories of losing your family."

Willow stiffened beneath his embrace for a moment and then nodded. "I have nothing but terrible memories from hospitals." She took a deep breath and sat up straight. "Enough of that. Let's get out of here and find a place to stay tonight. It's getting late, and I'm starving, so I know you've got to be, too."

And just like that, his strong Willow was back, taking charge of the situation and putting her emotions in check. Reaching out, he took her hand to help her up, but this time, he didn't let her pull away like she usually did and she didn't fight it. There was shared strength in their touch, a hum of awareness and energy that they both needed tonight. It might've felt like junior high to some people, but Jack liked having that connection with her.

He was suddenly desperate not to lose it. Tonight or maybe ever.

"I hope you like Thai food," Willow said as she unpacked a sack of takeout.

They'd found a nice hotel a block or so from the hospital that had availability and a room with two queen beds and a kitchenette. While Jack showered, Willow had gone in search of dinner and a pharmacy to pick up some essentials for the night. She'd returned about an hour later with toiletries and enough Thai food to feed an army. She'd followed her nose to a place down the street and if the scents were any indication, they were in for a treat. She hadn't had good Thai or even Chinese food in ages. It wasn't exactly an option on her tiny island.

Jack came out from the bathroom wearing only his sweatpants from earlier. His blond hair was still damp and curling at the edges, and the steam from the bathroom had left moist highlights along the ridges of his stomach and chest. Willow had to look away and tried to focus on setting out dinner instead.

"Thai food, huh? I don't know if I like it or if I've even had it before, but it sure smells good."

They settled down at the small table for two the room provided. The cartons and containers of various Thai delicacies took up nearly every inch of the table, leaving them barely enough room for their plates and the sodas she'd purchased at the pharmacy.

They were both exhausted from a long day and ate in relative silence for a while. Even in the quiet, however, Willow was aware of a change between them. Something had shifted today. She had always been attracted to him. And he'd kissed her, so she supposed he was into her on some level. But neither of them had really pressed the issue since that night on the couch.

But today, when he'd taken her hand outside the hospital, things changed. The attraction was still there, but there was more to it. An affection. A need to support and care for each other in a way that went far beyond an emotionless hookup. And it made things both easier and harder. It made her relax around him. She was far more comfortable with Jack than she'd been with anyone in years. Even on such a trying day. But that kind of comfort threatened the walls she'd built to protect herself. Before too long, she was certain she was going to let Jack get close to her. And when he left, it would leave a catastrophic mess in his wake.

Even so, she knew she couldn't resist him. She wanted to reach across the table and take his hand again. To feel his skin against her own. She felt not so alone with him there. It wasn't until that moment that she realized how miserable she really was on her island.

She thought she was protecting herself going out there. Convincing herself that all she needed was her books, her coffee and her dog. But it wasn't enough and she knew it. Having Jack around made it impossible to lie to herself any longer.

"Can I ask you something?" Jack finally spoke up as they finished their meal.

Willow sat back in her chair and pushed the half-eaten plate of pad Thai away before she ate more and made herself sick. "Sure." She was happy to get out of her own head and the turn her thoughts had taken.

"That first night we spent together...when the storm hit and the power went out. I kissed you and everything seemed to be going well until it wasn't. Did I do something wrong?"

Maybe her thoughts were safer. "No. Like I told you, I just realized it was a bad idea," Willow said as she got up and carried a few empty food cartons into the kitchenette.

Jack didn't let her escape the conversation so easily. He followed her with the last of their dinner and set it on the counter beside her. "Are you sure that's all it was?" he asked as he leaned against the counter. He was so near to her that her senses were flooded with the scent of his freshly washed skin and the heat of his body.

With a sigh, Willow turned to face him. The movement put her so close to him that they almost touched, but she felt childish taking a step back. "No, that wasn't all it was," she said, letting her gaze fall to his bare collarbone. "I panicked, okay? It had been a long time since I'd been attracted to someone and it felt like we were moving too fast."

Jack's hand came to rest at her waist. "Willow?" he asked softly.

She couldn't answer with him touching her like that. The hem of her shirt just barely brushed the waistband of her jeans, and his fingers had come to rest on a fraction of her bare skin. It was a simple touch, and yet it made her heart leap in her chest and her breath catch in her throat. He'd kept his distance since that first night, something that had both relieved and disappointed her. But he'd been a stranger then. And too injured to move. Now he was neither of those things. It was a question of if she could allow herself to open up to him.

"Yes?"

He slipped his finger under her chin and tilted her head up until she had no choice but to look at him. She felt her cheeks flush with embarrassment and excitement as her gaze met his. His brown eyes searched her face as his lips tipped upward in a smile of encouragement. "That's what I hoped."

Willow almost couldn't hear him for the blood rushing in her ears. Being here in Seattle seemed to be bringing their attraction to the surface, maybe because they both knew they were one step closer to losing their chance to be together. Eventually they would find out who he really was and he would return to his life. If this was their moment, they needed to take it.

"Why would you say that?" she asked.

Jack slid his hand around to her lower back, pulling her body flush against his own. "Because I've laid in bed alone each night thinking about that kiss we shared and worrying that I might not ever get to kiss you again because I screwed up somehow."

Willow gasped at his words. She'd never had a man say something like that to her before. Not even before she got sick and allowed herself the luxury of dating.

"I've fantasized about holding you in my arms again. I know that I shouldn't because I don't know anything about myself, or if I'm even good for you, but I can't help it. Now that we're off the island, it feels like I'm that much closer to leaving you and I don't like it. It makes me want to throw caution to the wind and not hold back anymore."

The longer he spoke, the more she fell under his spell. He was right. They were going to lose their chance and she would spend the rest of her life kicking herself for passing up the opportunity. Yes, she was ashamed of her body. But there had to be a way she could work around that and still get what she wanted. She had to.

"Then don't," she said, boldly meeting his eyes.

He narrowed his gaze at her for a moment. Then Jack's lips met hers without hesitation. His kiss was powerful yet not so overwhelming as to scare her off a second time. Willow stood on tiptoe to wrap her arms around his neck and draw herself closer to him. When his tongue sought hers out, she opened to him and melted into his touch.

She had thought the kiss in front of the fire was amazing, but that was nothing, nothing like this. This kiss was like a lightning bolt, shocking her dormant inner core back to life. As his hands rubbed her back and his fingers pressed greedily into her flesh, all she could think about was how badly she needed Jack.

"I want you," she whispered against his lips.

Jack broke away from her mouth and trailed kisses along her jawline to the sensitive hollow of her neck. "Whatever you want, it's yours," he said in a low growl at her ear.

His mouth returned to hers, hungrier than before. This was no longer just a simple kiss. They'd officially moved on to foreplay. Without breaking the kiss, he walked them backward through the little kitchenette until her legs met with the small dining room table where they'd just eaten. Willow eased up until she was sitting on it with Jack nestled snugly between her denim-clad thighs. She could feel his desire pressing against her, sending a shiver of need down her spine.

Jack slipped his hand beneath her shirt to stroke the smooth skin of her back and press her even closer to him. He moved to lift the hem and remove her T-shirt, but Willow grabbed his hand and stopped him.

"I need to leave it on. Please."

He frowned, confused by her hesitation, but he didn't argue with her.

"My chest is very…sensitive," she said. "I don't like having it touched." She left out why. She also left out that she was wearing one of her padded mastectomy bras to give her some shape where she no longer had any. "I'm sorry," she murmured, feeling the need to say something.

"Don't be sorry. If you don't like something, just tell me." Jack quickly moved on from her shirt, leaving it in place. She felt his hand slide down her stomach to her jeans instead. She lifted her hips as he slid them and her panties down her legs.

As he stood, his eyes devoured her long legs splayed out in front of him. He kissed her again and let his hand wander over her bare thigh as he did. Jack dipped his fingers between her legs, brushing over her sensitive skin and sending a shiver through her whole body.

He did it again, harder, and this time Willow cried aloud when he made contact. "Jack!"

Clearly encouraged by her response, he stroked again and again until she was panting and squirming at the edge of the table. He built up the release inside her so quickly, she could hardly believe it until it was almost too late.

"Stop," she gasped, gripping his wrist with her hand. "Not yet. I want you inside me."

"Very well," Jack agreed. His gaze never left hers

as he slipped out of his pants and kicked them aside. He settled back between her legs, and Willow felt him press against her.

"Yes," she hissed as he slowly sank into her.

He gripped her hips, holding her steady as he started to move in her. Every stroke set off fire bursts beneath her eyelids as they fluttered closed. Willow arched her back and braced her hands on the table as their movements became more desperate.

How had she even gotten here? This morning, she'd reluctantly boarded a ferry to escort Jack to the hospital. And now, she was having sex with Jack and on the verge of her first orgasm in ages. She could feel it building inside her. He coaxed the response from her body so easily, as though they were longtime lovers.

"So close," she said between ragged breaths.

Jack seemed to know just what to do to push her over the edge. Rolling his hips forward, he thrust harder, striking her sensitive core with each advance. In seconds, Willow was tensing up in anticipation of her undoing.

Then it hit. It radiated through her body like a nuclear blast. She clung to Jack's shoulders as the shock waves of pleasure made every muscle tremble and quiver. They rode through it together. With her final gasp, her head dropped back and her body went limp in his arms.

"Willow," he groaned, thrusting hard into her.

He surged forward and gasped against the curve of her throat as he poured into her.

Willow cradled him against her chest as he recovered, the sweat dampening the cotton and pressing it to her skin. Thoughts swirled through her mind as the sexual haze faded away and she realized what they'd just done. What she'd just done.

Before she could say anything, Jack straightened up and kissed her tenderly on the lips. "To the bedroom?" he asked.

Yes, a bed was exactly what they needed. Leaving their clothes where they lay, they made their way into the other area of the suite. They tugged the blankets down and curled up together in the plush, clean cotton. He tugged her back against him and wrapped his arms around her waist.

Willow was on the verge of falling asleep, content in his arms, when her cell phone rang. With a groan of displeasure, she rolled over and looked at the screen. It was the hospital.

"Hello?" she answered.

"Yes, can I speak with Mr. Jack Doe, please? This is Dr. Dunne with Harborview Medical."

She passed the phone over to Jack, who quietly conversed with the man for a few minutes. Willow was anxious to hear what they had to say. They'd called sooner than she expected. Hopefully it wasn't bad news. She wasn't sure she could face returning to the hospital tonight.

"What is it?" she asked as he hung up the phone.

Jack had a strange expression on his face as he looked at the phone and seemed to struggle with what he'd just heard.

"Are you okay? Did they find something serious?"

"I'm fine. Nothing more than we already expected."

Willow didn't understand. "Okay. Then what's wrong?"

He cleared his throat and passed the phone back to her. "First thing this morning, they took a photo of me with some basic information and sent it out to the Seattle police department to see if there was a match for any of their missing-person cases."

Willow's heart skipped in her chest. No. No. No. No. No. Not so soon. Not when things were so good between them. She'd never thought she'd have anything like she'd shared with Jack after beating cancer. She wasn't prepared to give it up yet. And somehow she knew that Jack's next words were going to change everything.

"They got a match almost immediately on a case reported to them yesterday. Apparently my twin brother is here in Seattle looking for me. And my name…is Finn Steele."

Six

Jack sat nervously at a diner booth with Willow beside him. They'd arranged to meet with the man claiming to be his twin—Sawyer Steele—for breakfast the following morning. He'd barely been able to sleep the night before and had already downed two cups of black coffee since they arrived. His feet anxiously tapped on the tile floor, his mind racing with the possibilities of meeting this man.

"Maybe you should switch to decaf, Jack. I mean, Finn? Maybe? This will be an adjustment."

"You're telling me." He'd hoped that hearing his real name would be enough to unlock his mind, but no luck. "Finn Steele" meant nothing to him. He felt more like Jack Doe than anything.

The door of the diner opened and a bell chimed to announce a customer. Both Jack and Willow looked up at once to see if it was the man they were expecting.

There was no question. The man standing at the entrance looked exactly like Jack. A rich, powerful, confident version of Jack he couldn't begin to relate to. Sawyer was tall, with the same blond curls in a different style. When the man turned and made contact with the same brown eyes, he smiled and rushed over to their table.

"Finn! Thank God."

Jack stood to greet the stranger, not expecting the violent hug that met him instead. He groaned with the pain of the impact, taking a step back as soon as he could to clutch his healing rib cage.

"Oh no, I hurt you. I'm sorry. They didn't tell me anything on the phone except that you had amnesia. Are you okay? I can't believe you're alive. They told us that you were dead, but I just couldn't believe it."

It was a lot coming at Jack all at once. He wasn't quite sure what to say to the man, so he held out his hand to gesture for him to sit across from them. He settled back into the booth beside Willow and clutched her hand for support beneath the tabletop. "I've got a few broken ribs. The bump on the head has been the biggest problem. I was pretty beat up in general when Willow found me. I felt like hell for a couple days, but it's better now. Thanks to Willow's expert care, of course."

Sawyer finally turned to acknowledge the silent woman sitting beside Jack. He smiled at her and looked back at his brother. "I should've known that no matter what situation you'd gotten into, you'd find a beautiful woman to care for you."

"Excuse me?" Jack asked. He didn't like the man's tone. Or rather, he didn't like what his tone said about Jack. Perhaps he was more than just a flirt.

"Wow. You really don't remember anything. Nothing at all?"

"Nothing personal. I don't know who I am, or what I was like. I certainly don't know how I ended up on that beach."

Sawyer's brow went up in surprise. "You washed up on a beach?"

"We're not sure," Willow said, finally speaking up. "I found him unconscious on the beach not far from my house on Shaw Island. It's part of the San Juan Islands off the coast here."

Sawyer shook his head in amazement. "That's wild. That's got to be more than two hundred miles from where the plane finally went down."

Jack sat upright, his brother's words a surprise. He'd imagined a dozen ways he could've ended up on that beach and none of them had involved a plane crash. "You're saying I was on a plane?"

"Yes. You were flying back from Beijing on a corporate jet. They're still not sure what happened, but there was an explosion. I guess maybe you were sucked out of the plane over the ocean before it went down in the national forest lands. The crash investigators were insistent that you were dead even when we couldn't find your body because you could've ended up anywhere. Honestly, until I saw you just now, I was worried they were right. It's a miracle you survived."

Jack had been given so much information and yet the pieces still weren't coming together in his mind. He couldn't quite believe that he'd survived a plane crash any more than he could believe he was used to flying on private jets and traveling to China. None of this life Sawyer described seemed like it could be his. "Can you tell me who I am?" he asked. "You're obviously my twin brother, but what else should I know?"

Sawyer nodded and gave him a soft, understanding smile that made Jack like him a little more than before. "It's a lot to absorb, I know. I shouldn't have thrown it at you all at once, but seeing you sitting here…" He shook his head and blinked away a shimmer of glassy tears in his eyes. "Your name is Finn Hamilton Steele. Hamilton is our mother's maiden name. You live in Charleston, South Carolina. Our whole family lives there. You and I are both vice presidents for the family company, Steele Tools, which was founded by our great-grandfather and is currently run by our father, Trevor Steele."

"Steele Tools, as in the company that makes the hammers and screwdrivers you can find in almost every home in the country?" Willow asked.

Sawyer nodded. "Yes. If you haven't already guessed, Finn, you're also ridiculously rich."

The waitress chose that moment to arrive at their table. They all forced themselves to order breakfast and coffee, sending her away as fast as possible.

"Ridiculously rich?" Jack said the words aloud, but he couldn't quite grasp the idea. He was wearing a five-dollar T-shirt from the Shaw Island General Store that Willow had had to buy for him. He didn't have a solitary dime in his pocket. "Are you sure?"

"Unless you've managed to blow your entire billion-dollar trust fund on women and sports cars, then yes. I don't think even you could waste money that quickly."

Jack got a sinking feeling in his gut. For anyone else, hearing that he was a billionaire likely would've been good news. But he couldn't help but home in on his brother's words: "women and sports cars." It made him sound like he was some kind of wild playboy. He'd known almost immediately that he had a great fondness for women, but Sawyer made it sound as though he had a different one on his arm every week or something.

"Am I married?" He held his breath, hoping the answer was no. It didn't sound like he was, but who knew? Perhaps he wasn't Mr. Monogamy. But he didn't want to be that guy. If he was married and didn't know it, his romance with Willow couldn't be held against him, but he still didn't like the idea of it.

"Ah, no. You're not married. Not even close. You proposed to my wife earlier this year, but she turned you down. That's the closest you've gotten to the altar."

Jack frowned. That sentence didn't even make sense. He decided to ignore it and focus in on the fact that no, he hadn't cheated on his wife with Willow. He was free to be with her if he wanted to.

He took a deep breath and finally started to relax into the booth. He wasn't a criminal. He wasn't married. It was a relief to know he hadn't drawn Willow into some messy intrigue by making love to her last night. He could deal with anything else he found out about himself just knowing that much was true.

"So, Finn, huh?" Jack gritted his teeth as he said it. The name—like the rest of his new identity—felt like wearing someone else's shoes, but he'd have to get over it.

"Our dad loved Mark Twain's stories when he was growing up, and all of us are named after different characters from his books. Our older brother is Tom. Then there's you and me and our younger sister Morgan. He got her name from *A Connecticut Yankee in King Arthur's Court*. Oh, and we also have a sister named Jade, which has nothing to do with Mark Twain, but that's a long story for another day."

He didn't doubt it. Everything about his life seemed impossibly complicated. It made him want to go back to Shaw Island and hide out with Willow forever.

"They're all going to be thrilled when I tell them the news. I didn't want to say anything until I knew for sure that I'd really found you. Mother has been a wreck. They'll want you home as soon as possible. I took one of the company jets here to look for you, but you don't have to worry about flying home. After the crash, we had a crew of technicians go over each one in the fleet. It's perfectly safe." Sawyer turned to Willow. "I'm sure you'll be glad to get this guy out of your hair. I can't imagine taking in someone who has no clue who they are or how they got there, but you're a good person. There's a reward for information about Finn. Our parents will happily pay it to compensate you for the inconvenience of it all."

"I don't need any money." Willow had been tense and mostly quiet since Sawyer had walked in. Now Jack could almost feel the waves of irritation coming off of her. She wasn't happy about any of this, and frankly, neither was he.

It would all be so much easier if his memory

would return. Then his whole life wouldn't feel like he was reading someone else's biography.

"When would we leave?" Jack asked.

"As soon as you're ready."

Jack looked at the beautiful woman beside him and wasn't sure he would ever be ready.

"I want you to come with me."

Willow stopped in her tracks just inside their hotel room and turned to face Jac—*Finn*. After breakfast, Sawyer had returned to his suite at the Four Seasons to call family. This was their first chance to speak privately since the bomb of his identity had been dropped on them both.

"What do you mean come with you? Where? To the Four Seasons?" He was supposed to be meeting his brother there later to make plans to return home.

"No. To Charleston. I want you to come back with me."

Finn—*right on the first try, finally*—had to be out of his mind. "What reason do I have to go to South Carolina? You're going home to your family and your old life. You don't need me there."

He shut the hotel room door and closed the space between them. He wrapped his arms around her waist and pulled her close, his scent wearing away at her resolve. "That's where you're wrong. I do need you there. Just like yesterday at the hospital—I need your support to get through this. These people might be my family, but I don't know them. Right now, you," he said, looking into her eyes, "are my whole world. I can't remember a time when you weren't in my life." Finn smiled. "Don't make me do this without you."

Willow knew she would eventually relent—she couldn't tell him no when he looked at her like that—but she had to voice her concerns first. "I grew up dirt-poor on a commune. I don't know the first thing about how to act around rich people. I'll embarrass myself and you in the process."

"I could never be embarrassed by you," he insisted. "And I'm in the same boat. I don't remember anything about my life. I don't feel like a billionaire. Sawyer could've said I was a circus clown and I would shrug and go along with it because it all feels wrong to me anyway. But all that talk of being a vice president and having trust funds… I feel like this is all some cruel prank being played on me. The only truth, the only constant in my life right now, is you. You're my lifeline, Willow Bates."

It was nice to be needed, but Willow could feel the anxiety tickling at the back of her brain. She was going with him to help ease the transition. No more, no less. She shouldn't expect anything other than a week together. But she couldn't help but feel a bit used. "And when you're comfortable in your old life again? When you get your memories back?

What then? I come home to Washington and we pretend like none of this ever happened?"

"No, of course not." Finn ran his palms reassuringly along the backs of her arms. "I'm not sure what I'm walking into here, but we'll figure things out as we go. I'm not ready to give this—you—up yet. But under the circumstances, we can't promise each other anything, either. All I can tell you is that if you get there and you don't like it, you can leave whenever you want. I won't ask you to stay. But go with me."

Finn reached up to brush a honey-gold strand of hair from her eyes. "Please."

"I'll see if Doc can keep Shadow," she said with a heavy sigh of resignation. "But I'm not staying more than a week no matter what. I have a life, a deadline. And I won't impose on Doc any longer than I have to."

"A week is perfect." Finn grinned and the single dimple in his cheek appeared, tempting her to lean in and kiss it.

She watched him for a moment before giving in to the urge and pressing her lips first to his dimple, and then to his lips. "I think Finn suits you. It's sort of a mischievous name. Like that smile of yours."

He shrugged. "It's growing on me. It could've been worse."

Willow pulled away and looked around the hotel room. "Well, we need to check out if I'm going to make the next ferry. I'll talk to Doc, pack a bag and then meet you and Sawyer at the Four Seasons. Okay?"

He nodded. "Just don't take too long. Sawyer has threatened to take me shopping this afternoon."

She looked him over, eyeing the clothes she'd bought him that first night. It certainly wasn't what you'd expect some tool magnate to wear. "You could probably use some clothes that don't say San Juan Islands on them. Speaking of which, is there anything you left at the house that I should pack for you?" He certainly hadn't left for Seattle thinking he wouldn't return.

Finn looked thoughtful for a moment and then shook his head. "The only thing I need is you."

Willow rolled her eyes dramatically and laughed. "I've already agreed to go. No need to lay it on so thick."

They gathered up what little they had in the room and left. She put Finn in a cab to the Four Seasons and caught another to the ferry pier.

Being away from Finn, alone on the boat, gave Willow time to think. Perhaps too much time. The whole way back to Shaw Island, she wondered if she were crazy to go with him.

This whole time, she'd thought he was a Seattle executive or something. Smart and well-to-do, definitely, but a billionaire? The heir of a tool empire that was a household name? That was beyond her wildest imaginings. Whatever girlish fantasies she might've entertained about the two of them together were dashed the instant she heard who he really was.

Jack and Willow made sense. Finn and Willow didn't stand a chance.

Maybe she was just fooling herself by going to Charleston. She was clinging to a dream that had died the moment Sawyer walked in the door of that diner. But she couldn't help herself. Despite believing it to be impossible, she'd allowed herself to develop feelings for Finn. All she could do now was make the most of every moment she could with him. And when it was over, it would hurt, but it would be worth it.

Willow had a week left with Finn. And a lifetime to hold on to the memories and hope that was enough.

"I'm sorry, could you repeat that?" Kat said with a near-hysterical edge to her voice.

Sawyer grinned and repeated his words loud and clear for his wife to understand over the phone. "He's alive, Kat. I knew he hadn't died in the plane crash and I was right. I found him."

He didn't have to be with her in Charleston to know that the stunned silence on the end of the line was being caused by her quiet tears. Third-trimester hormones were getting the best of her lately. She cried at television commercials. Social media posts. Surely this news would start the waterworks, as well, so he continued to talk and take the pressure to speak off of her.

"He ended up on an island, hundreds of miles away from the crash."

"Is he okay?"

"For the most part, but he did hit his head. We would've found him sooner if he had any clue who he was or how he washed up on that beach."

There was a moment of hesitation before Kat spoke. "Are you saying Finn has *amnesia*?"

"I know, it sounds crazy, but it's true. He's been staying with a woman for the last few days and going by the name Jack. He has no clue who he is, who I am or anything about his life before the plane crash."

Kat made a thoughtful sound on the line. "Are you sure… I mean, he couldn't be faking it, could he? Not the wreck, obviously, but could the amnesia be a ploy to try and take advantage of a little free time without responsibilities or your father hulking over his shoulder?"

Sawyer had considered that, but even Finn had limits on how low he would sink. "He's absolutely not faking it. And you know how I know?"

"How?"

"Because he's completely smitten with the woman that rescued him."

There was another long silence. "Finn is…smitten?"

"I can't think of a better word to use, but yeah.

Smitten, infatuated, whatever you want to call it. He sat across the table from me at breakfast practically beaming at her the whole time. Holding her hand. I haven't seen him act that way with a woman in my entire life. Not even some good old teenage puppy love back in high school."

"This I've got to see."

Sawyer took a deep breath. "Well, you're going to get your chance. Because Finn insists on bringing her back to Charleston with him. At least for a week or so."

The news had nearly knocked Sawyer off his feet, but when Finn had arrived at the hotel, he announced that Willow would be meeting them tonight and traveling back with them to South Carolina. This was so unlike his brother, Sawyer almost couldn't believe it was really Finn, if he hadn't been the spitting image of his twin.

Finn liked everything in his life to be flashy and beautiful, be it women, cars, watches…everything. But he kept the cars and the watches far longer than the women. He adored them all, but was easily bored by them and certainly wasn't interested in the long-term care and maintenance that one required.

If he was honest, this woman, Willow, was pretty enough. She had a tiny frame, very slender, and was almost swallowed by the cardigan she wore over her T-shirt. She wasn't wearing a stitch of makeup. Her blond hair was cut short, which made her eyes seem even bigger than they were. Her face was interesting with high cheekbones and full lips that were in contrast to her lack of curves anywhere else. She wasn't what you could call traditionally beautiful, but she was the kind of oddly attractive woman you would see on a high-fashion magazine cover or catwalk.

That was not his brother's type. At all. He liked curves, flowing hair, lots of makeup and tight clothes. He liked them high-maintenance and fun to drive, like his cars. Willow was quiet, but smart and well-spoken. She seemed thoughtful and genuinely concerned for his brother without knowing anything about who he was and what he could offer her. It was refreshing, if not a little disconcerting.

"He really did hit his head hard, didn't he?" Kat noted.

"Absolutely. And it's not just her. There's a complete personality change in him. He's not as outspoken or extroverted. He isn't constantly making jokes or sarcastic comments. He actually seemed to be really serious about the whole situation. Which, of course, is not like him at all."

"Well, I can't wait to see how all this turns out. Where is he now?"

"He's in the bathroom taking a shower and cleaning up. I hauled him down to Neiman Marcus and bought him some clothes so he would at least look like himself when he arrived back in Charleston.

Mother would faint if she saw him in the sweatpants and flip-flops he had on this morning."

Kat chuckled and followed up her laugh with an "oh" sound. "The baby kicked. She must think that's funny, too."

Sawyer smiled, picturing his wife and her large, round belly as she sat in the wingback chair. Lately it was the only chair in the house she could get up out of on her own. He hated leaving her and the baby, especially when they were getting so close to her arrival. But finding his brother was important. Finn was the baby's biological father, after all. Having him be a part of the baby's life was just as vital as having Sawyer around.

"I think she misses you," Kat said. "And so do I. When will you guys be coming back?"

"We may wait until the morning. I have to talk to the pilot and see what he recommends with the weather and flight time. We also have to wait for Willow to return to Seattle on the ferry."

The bedroom door of the suite opened and Finn walked into the room in his new suit. It wasn't as well tailored as it should be, but under the circumstances, it would do.

"I need to let you go. I'll see you soon. I love you."

"I love you, too," Kat said.

Sawyer hung up the phone and looked at his

brother. He looked like Finn. Sounded like Finn. But he certainly didn't act like him.

Maybe, Sawyer thought, that wasn't all bad.

Seven

The moment Willow stepped onto the Steele corporate jet, she knew she was woefully unprepared for this trip. The small jet sat six guests in plush leather seats, three on each side of the aisle. At the top of the stairs, they were greeted by their flight attendant, an attractive, middle-aged brunette named Gloria, who offered them each a glass of champagne as they boarded.

"I'm so glad to know you're safe, Mr. Steele," Gloria said as she gave Finn a crystal flute of golden liquid. "I knew I had to break out our best bubbly to celebrate your return home."

"I was sorry to hear about the others," he responded, with a sober expression on his face.

Willow had learned the night before that two pilots, a flight attendant and another passenger had lost their lives when the jet crashed. Considering the state of the wreck Sawyer described, it really was a miracle that Finn had survived. The best they could guess was that he was wearing one of the plane's parachutes when the explosion tore the fuselage in half.

Gloria looked pleasantly surprised at Finn's thoughtful words and nodded. "It's a risk we accept and hope to not face in our line of work," she said. "But no worries about today. This jet has been fully vetted by the best mechanics and inspectors in the business."

"Thankfully, I don't remember the crash," Finn said. "Or anything else for that matter. So I'll be fine."

"Well, just in case, I do have some Xanax if anyone needs it."

At first, Willow thought Gloria was kidding, but when no one laughed, she accepted her drink and kept her mouth shut. The world really did work differently for the rich in ways she never even imagined.

She settled into a seat in the second row across the aisle from Finn. Putting her champagne into the polished wood cup holder, she nervously buckled her seat belt. Then, she picked up the glass and downed it all in one gulp. It was probably a waste of very good champagne, but she didn't care at the moment.

"Are you afraid of flying?" Finn asked. He was relaxing casually in his seat as though he hadn't nearly died in a plane like this less than a week ago.

"No. I've flown a couple times in my life. Coach, of course. But if I wasn't afraid before, meeting you would change that. I'm just a bit of an anxious traveler. I've spent too much time as a homebody, I think."

That wasn't entirely a lie. She never had traveled much. She had a passport, but only to go over to Canada from time to time. But really, her anxiety had kicked in the moment she met the brothers in the Four Seasons lobby. Both of them were standing there waiting for her, looking incredibly handsome. One was wearing a navy suit and the other a black suit. It was amazing how much they looked alike standing side by side smiling at her. At least until she noticed they each had a single dimple, but on opposite cheeks, like a mirror image of one another. Once she saw that, she knew that despite the new suit and the haircut, the one in black was Finn.

The fact that he wasn't wearing a tie should've given it away, but she knew for certain when he approached her and said hello with a firm kiss on the lips.

From there, things had been like one big wealthy

whirlwind. It started with the beautiful brass-and-marble lobby of the hotel and the two-bedroom hotel suite that was bigger than her first apartment. Then Sawyer treated them to dinner at the nicest seafood place in Seattle and ordered a bottle of wine that cost more than her mortgage. She'd had her first ride in a limousine when their car took them to the executive airport this morning.

And now, she was on a private jet, sipping a re-filled glass of champagne and wishing she'd had nicer clothes to pack. She had a few business pieces that she wore to author events and mystery conventions from time to time. Today, she'd chosen a black sheath dress with a cashmere sweater and ballet flats. It was a stretchy fabric and good for travel, but it didn't feel nice enough. She felt more like the secretary traveling with her CEO boss.

Willow imagined it would only get worse once they landed in Charleston.

She was halfway through her second glass of champagne when the jet started to taxi down the runway for takeoff. Minutes later, they were in the air without much trouble. It was a remarkably smooth ride. Once they leveled off, a chime sounded. The flight attendant got up and went to the back of the plane to do something in the galley.

In front of her, Sawyer pushed a button and rotated his seat around to face them. Reaching down between them, he pulled out a table that extended from the side and offered a large new space for Willow and Sawyer to set their drinks, paperwork or whatever else they might have with them.

"So, now that you're on the plane and you can't get away, I need to tell you about something."

Finn narrowed his eyes at his brother. "What could it possibly be? You've already warned me that your wife is pregnant with my baby. What could be worse than that?"

Willow sat stunned for a moment. She hadn't heard anything about a baby, much less one the brothers shared. She'd presumed, ignorantly, that when Finn didn't have a wife, that he didn't have children. Apparently that wouldn't be the case for much longer.

"It's a long story," Sawyer said to her with a comforting pat on the knee. "And it isn't necessarily worse news. Just not the kind that you would normally want to hear."

Finn sighed and sat back in his seat. "Okay, tell me."

"Well, you will soon learn, if you don't remember, that Mother likes to throw parties. We're always being summoned to the family home for big soirees. Charity events, weddings, garden parties for one thing or another. She lives for it. And once I told her you were flying back today, she started planning a welcome-home party for you Saturday night."

Finn didn't bat an eye. "What's so bad about that?

It seems like a nice-enough gesture. I won't know anyone there, but maybe meeting them will jog my memory."

Sawyer shook his head. "You don't get it. This isn't going to be twenty folks gathering to shake your hand and have nibbles and cocktails. When Mother throws a party, it's always a catered event for at least a hundred people. There will be an orchestra playing. It will be black-tie, for sure. If the weather holds up, it will be in the gardens. Otherwise she'll have it in the ballroom."

Willow groaned inwardly. His parents' home had a ballroom? She definitely hadn't packed the right outfit for that. She didn't have any beaded gowns in her closet and if she did, they would have husky hair on them. She wasn't sure what she was going to do. Maybe one of his sisters was short and flat chested and could loan her a dress? She doubted it.

Finn seemed equally startled by the news. "Are you serious?"

"As a heart attack," Sawyer said flatly. "She's been wanting to show off that ballroom, so I bet she has it inside no matter what. She had the whole thing redone after it was blown up last year, but Morgan had an outdoor wedding, and Kat and I eloped in Hawaii, so she hasn't had a chance yet."

"Did you just say someone blew up the ballroom?" Willow asked. The craziest statements seemed to roll off Sawyer's tongue like they were everyday occurrences for normal people.

"Well, he wasn't very successful, but he did enough damage that Mother had an excuse to redecorate."

"Do people normally try to blow up our family?" Finn asked. "This seems like something I should know."

"No, that was new. Honestly, things were pretty normal with our family until we found out that our little sister had been switched at birth. We grew up with Morgan, but our biological sister is Jade. The guy that tried to kidnap and ransom Jade as a baby tried again last year, and when it didn't work out again, the guy posed as a caterer and tried to blow us all up."

Both Willow and Finn sat in stunned silence. The awkwardness was only broken by Gloria approaching everyone with individual plates of fresh fruit and croissants. At this point, Willow was happy to get something in her stomach to go with the champagne. Her head was starting to swim, and given the current conversation, she might say something rude. Were the lives of all rich people like a big soap opera?

"Anyway," Sawyer continued, "no one was hurt. And things worked out in the end. But I'm telling you, Mother's itching to have people over. She had to get off the phone with me last night so she could start making calls. Don't be surprised if there are two hundred people there to see the infamous Finn Steele return from the dead."

Finn looked at Willow and put a grape wordlessly into his mouth. She could tell from his expression that he was just as blown away by the conversation as she was. Only for him, this was regular life. He couldn't remember it, but there had been a time not long ago where he could speak about his family without batting an eye, too. It made Willow's family seem tragic and boring by comparison.

"Gloria?" Finn spoke up, turning to the back of the jet, where the flight attendant was working in the galley. "I think I'm going to need that Xanax."

"Don't leave me," Willow whispered between the gritted teeth of a feigned smile. "I don't care what anyone says or does, please stay with me."

"I was going to say the same thing to you," Finn admitted. "Aren't we a pair?"

Finn looked up at the huge antebellum mansion in front of them. It was massive with two-story columns and dark shutters that stood out against the stark white limestone. Coming down the long driveway lined with moss-covered live oak trees had been intimidating enough, but this? How could this possibly be his childhood home? It seemed impossible.

The doors flew open and Finn clutched Willow's hand. A few women around their age came out first—a blonde, a brunette and a redhead—the redhead visibly pregnant. Some men followed behind them. One had to be his brother Tom based on the resemblance. The others must be his sisters' husbands, because they were both big, dark, bearded and completely unlike the Steele men in every way. An older couple, presumably his parents, came out behind them, followed last by a tiny old woman who looked more like the Queen of England than old Elizabeth Windsor herself.

The crowd rushed forward at once. It was a cacophony of words and hugs and tears, most of which Finn could barely understand. He stood stiffly, accepting each embrace as everyone said their hellos, but not really reciprocating. The only one to keep their distance was the old woman still on the porch, leaning on her cane.

"You all are going to scare him to death. The boy doesn't know you from Adam. Look at his bewildered face. Don't smother him."

Everyone took a step back and Finn made note of who really ran this place. He would guess it was Grandma.

"Come in," she said, gesturing inside. "It's hot as blue blazes out here."

Still holding Willow's hand, Finn walked toward the house with the others in their wake. Inside the mansion was equally imposing. A large, grand staircase greeted guests as they entered beneath a sparkling crystal chandelier.

It was all very nice. And about as unfamiliar as the Palace of Versailles. Finn swallowed his frustration as he crossed the foyer. He'd hoped that coming back here would jog his memory. The people he'd just met were supposedly the most important people in his life. His family. He was in the home where he'd grown up. And yet he might as well have been anywhere, meeting any new group of strangers.

At least he had Willow here with him. He looked at her and tried to smile reassuringly. She seemed to be just as nervous as he was about all of this. But she was here. His rock when he needed her the most. He'd never be able to properly thank her for her support. Not even with all the money he supposedly had in his accounts. But he'd have to find a way.

They followed the old woman as she clicked across the marble floors with her cane to a large family room.

"Have a seat," she said as she lowered herself into a velvet wingback chair fit for a queen.

Finn chose a love seat, putting Willow beside him and keeping the others at a comfortable distance. Almost immediately, an older woman he hadn't met yet arrived and offered them both tall glasses of sweet iced tea. She also placed a platter of cookies and finger sandwiches onto the coffee table in front of them. When she was done, she reached out and cupped Finn's face for a moment, tears in her eyes.

"Welcome home, Finn," she said, and then disappeared from the room as quickly as she'd arrived.

"Who was that?" Finn asked.

"That's Lena, the housekeeper. She took your accident especially hard. She's wonderful, been with the family since the children were young. Since *you* were young," his grandmother corrected. "I think you may be her favorite."

Once everyone was seated, they took turns introducing themselves in a slower fashion he might actually be able to keep up with. The older woman was his paternal grandmother, Ingrid Steele. His parents, Trevor and Patricia, were seated on the sofa. His brother Tom lurked in the corner nibbling on a cookie and saying very little. He looked more like their father than he or Sawyer did.

The woman with platinum-blonde hair like Patricia was his biological sister, Jade. The petite accountant was in sharp contrast to the massive man hovering around her—her husband, Harley. He was some kind of former military security specialist and he looked the part. The dark-haired woman with the dark-haired man were his sister Morgan and her husband, River, a real estate developer. She had left the family company to start her own charity for premature babies the year before. Lastly, there was the redhead sitting beside Sawyer. Kat. She was a woodcarving artist. She was also seven months pregnant with his daughter, Beatrice.

If he recognized any of them, he thought it would be her. The woman he'd seduced and accidentally impregnated while pretending to be his brother. It was such an incredibly shitty story to hear about himself. But he tried to tell himself that things had worked out. Kat had married Sawyer and they were blissfully happy. If the baby looked like Finn, that meant it would look just like Sawyer, as well.

It did worry him, though. How many other stories were there where he was an asshole? It sounded like he went through women like tissues. It didn't feel like that's who he really was. But they would know better than he would. The more Finn learned about his life before the plane crash, the less he wanted to regain his memory. Maybe it was better if he didn't and could just start his life fresh.

"And who is this young lady?" his mother asked once everyone else had been introduced.

"This is the woman that saved my life." Finn squeezed her hand and looked at her with appreciation in his eyes. "Everyone, this is Willow Bates. She's a mystery writer that just happened to live in the middle of nowhere where I turned up. I don't know what would've happened if she hadn't found me and taken such good care of me."

"Wait a minute," Jade said. "Are you S. W. Bates? The author of the Amelia Mysteries? I love those books. I have about a dozen."

"That's me. S. W. Bates is the pen name I use. If

you bring one of the books by, I'll be happy to autograph it for you."

Finn seemed surprised by the whole exchange. He knew she wrote books and did well enough, but he didn't know she and her characters were recognizable names in the genre. "What does *S.W.* stand for?" Finn asked.

Willow looked at him with a touch of hesitation lining her brow. "My initials, is all."

"Willow isn't your first name?"

"No, but I've gone by Willow for many years now."

There was something about her expression that urged Finn not to press forward. She was embarrassed of her name, perhaps. He understood that, coming from a whole clan of Mark Twain characters. So, he'd let it go. For now. But eventually, he'd find out what that *S* stood for.

"Well, we can't thank you enough for what you did for our Finn. We really did think we'd lost him along with the others. We were making the final arrangements when Sawyer called and told us that he'd found you in Seattle." Patricia's eyes were blurred with tears as she spoke. "I couldn't believe it. You're his miracle."

Willow shifted uncomfortably. "Finn's surviving the fall was the miracle. I don't know how he ended up on my beach, but all I did was take him home and call a doctor."

"And get me medicine and clothes, and feed me and take care of me," Finn added.

Willow only shrugged. "It was what any decent person would do in that situation."

"Somehow I doubt that, but you've more than earned the reward we advertised for finding Finn."

"I don't need any reward."

"Posh," Patricia said dismissively. "You'll take that hundred grand and do something swell with it. Buy a boat. Pay down your mortgage. Give it to orphans. But you'll take it."

Finn glanced over at Willow, who seemed mildly irritated but not enough so to argue with his mother on the subject.

Patricia continued on, unfazed. "I'm sure Sawyer has told you about the welcome-home party I've been planning for you Saturday night," his mother said to the two of them. "It came together quickly, but I think it's really going to be a lovely affair. And considering everything you just said, I think Willow should also be a guest of honor at the party as the person who saved Finn. People will be so pleased to meet you, as well."

He could feel Willow tense beside him. Finn knew very little about himself, but he'd grown so familiar with Willow that he could read her like one of her books. Every flinch, every sigh, every gasp of pleasure… He knew exactly what was going on in her mind. So he spoke up.

"I'm not so sure it's the best idea right now. It's awfully soon after the accident. I'm still in a lot of pain and my memory hasn't returned. Maybe we could push it out a little bit. I'm not sure I'm ready to face all those people."

"Nonsense," Patricia said with a dismissive wave of her elegant fingers. "Everyone is dying to see you and we have to celebrate while Willow is still here in Charleston. A party might be just what you need to shake out the cobwebs in your brain."

"I also don't think Willow packed for that kind of event, Mother. I had no idea about the party until after we'd left."

"We can take her shopping," Morgan offered brightly. "We'll have a girls' day out, just Willow, Jade, Kat and I."

"That's a great idea," Jade added. "We'll get to know her better and we'll help her pick out something just right for the party."

"It can be our gift to you," Kat said. "For keeping Finn safe. A beautiful dress for a beautiful lady."

"I don't know," Finn began. It sounded like it could be overwhelming for her to spend the day with the girls. Never mind him having to go it alone all afternoon while she was shopping.

"It's okay," Willow said. "That sounds nice. They can probably do a better job helping me pick out a dress than you could."

"Yes, Finn's much better at taking them off than putting them on," someone quipped. Maybe Tom.

Finn sighed as the others tittered with laughter. He was getting tired of those comments. Even if he deserved them, there had to be more to his life than his pursuit of women. Being a rich playboy couldn't have taken up all his time, could it?

"I do hope you two will consider staying here for a few days. Upstairs there's a whole wing of the house that's empty now that all the children are gone. It will be very private, and you won't have to worry about cooking or cleaning with Lena here to handle things."

"Mom, Finn owns his own place just a few miles from here," Sawyer argued. "It might be better for him to spend time in a familiar environment. Being surrounded by his own things might be what brings his memories back."

"And I don't want to be underfoot," Finn added. "I'd really like to see my place. You're right, the more of my life I'm exposed to the better. That's what the doctors said," he lied.

In truth, he would go anywhere he could have time alone with Willow. He'd barely gotten to touch her since they'd made love that night at the hotel. Once he'd gotten the call from the hospital, it had been all drama and personal revelations. They'd shared a bed in Sawyer's suite the night before, but it had felt awkward to do more than spoon with his brother so nearby.

He didn't care if it was his place, or a hotel, or the garden shed in the yard; he just wanted some privacy. And to stroke Willow's soft skin. To talk her out of wearing that shirt so he could worship every inch of her. She'd made noises about being sensitive, and in the heat of the moment, he hadn't wanted to argue. But they couldn't go on like this forever. Whatever she was hiding from him, he wished she'd share it with him. And she wouldn't with his family lurking around.

"Well, if the doctor said so," Patricia relented. "But don't be a stranger around here."

Sawyer looked over at Finn and winked conspiratorially. Finn was really beginning to like his brother.

Eight

"You're so petite," Morgan remarked. "Anything will look good on you, like Jade and her ballerina's figure."

The three sisters had gotten Willow up early the next day and taken her to King Street in Downtown Charleston where all the high-end boutiques and department stores were located. She'd been hesitant to leave Finn, but if she didn't want to make a fool of herself at this party, she needed his sisters to help her get ready.

So far things had gone well, but she was a little overwhelmed. The women gave no notice to price tags or sales. They just picked up whatever they liked, making Willow thankful that they'd offered to buy her dress as a thank-you. She wouldn't even pay these prices for a wedding gown. Not that she'd ever need one.

"But you've got curves," Jade complained and clutched her barely B-cup chest. "I would've killed for your boobs in high school. Hell, I would kill for them *now*."

"Boobs are overrated," Morgan said.

"I doubt River would agree with that statement," Jade replied with a knowing grin.

"Well, neither of you have to buy a maternity gown today, so I don't want to hear it. I was hoping to get through this pregnancy without having to dress up. Now I'm going to look like a giant disco ball or a humpback whale in a beaded dress."

"I think a killer whale would be appropriate since it's black-tie attire," Morgan quipped.

Kat gave Morgan a cutting glance. "I will hurt you."

Willow listened to Finn's sisters all bicker at each other like old girlfriends. None of them were related by blood or had even grown up together as true sisters, and yet they had an amazing friendship. Her relationship with her own sister was strained and nothing like this at all. Their banter was amusing to listen to, but it was also a lot to keep up with. Especially knowing that a changing room and partial states of undress were looming in her future. She didn't imagine these ladies had a lot of boundaries. She was wearing her padded mastectomy bra and hoped it was enough to cover the scars and divert any questions.

"Ladies, these dresses seem a little over the top for me." Willow glanced at a price tag and winced. "I know you said it was a gift, but I'm not comfortable letting you pay this much for a dress I'll only wear once."

Kat and Jade looked at each other with a knowing glance.

"You're new at this," Kat said, putting a comforting hand on her shoulder. "We used to be in the same boat, Jade and I, so take our advice. Rule number one, Steeles don't look at price tags. Rule number two, quality and style are paramount because everyone is expecting it from you. The sooner you accept it, the easier it will be. So don't give it a second thought. You have to look good."

"What about this one?" Jade asked, holding up a strapless pale pink gown and turning the subject away from the ridiculous amount of money they were looking to spend.

That dress would never work. Even if she could find a strapless mastectomy bra in time, she couldn't hide the scar from her chemo port, which had yet to fade. "I think I'd prefer something with straps or sleeves. Maybe a high neckline. Something a little more modest. I like the color, though."

"Next thing you'll want a matching beaded bolero," Kat said. "Too modest and you'll end up in the same dress as Patricia. We can't have that. Especially under the circumstances."

"What circumstances?" Willow asked.

"Finn's favorite color is red," Morgan said, pointedly ignoring her question. "She should wear red if she's out to seal the deal."

Willow's eyes widened. Those circumstances. "Oh, I'm not out to—"

"He doesn't even know what his favorite color is," Kat interrupted. "But his Ferrari is red, so you probably can't go wrong with that. It's a statement-making color, for sure."

He drove a red Ferrari? Even after their long discussion the day before, Patricia had gotten her way and they'd stayed at the family home overnight. Today, after the shopping trip, they would go to Finn's townhome for the first time. And apparently, they would see his Ferrari and the other personal aspects of Finn's past that neither of them expected.

"I don't understand how amnesia works, I guess. He remembers basic things, but nothing personal? He can count to a hundred and tie his shoes, but doesn't remember any of us?" Morgan asked no one in particular. She narrowed her gaze at Willow for a moment and took a deep breath as she clutched a black beaded dress in her hands. "Okay, I'm going to ask the hard question, Willow. You and my brother are...*together*, right?"

"Morgan!" Jade chastised.

"It's a valid question," Morgan argued. "You've seen how they are with each other. Have you ever seen him like that with a woman before? No. So there's something to it. There has to be. Or there will be soon if we get the right dress."

All three sisters were suddenly silent and turned to look at Willow expectantly.

"It's complicated," she said. That was an understatement. Getting involved with someone in Finn's condition was asking for trouble.

"But you guys have...?" Kat wiggled her eyebrows suggestively.

"Yes, we have. But I doubt much more will come of it than that." It was a hard truth to speak aloud, but she needed to hear it as much as they did. Thankfully, they hadn't asked if she had feelings for him. That would be a more painful conversation with an equally doomed ending.

"So with amnesia, then," Morgan continued, "did he know what he was doing when you guys were together? I mean it should've been like his first time, right? Like being back in high school again or something. Or is it like riding a bike?"

"Morgan!" Jade repeated.

Morgan only shrugged and ignored her sister. "I'm just trying to figure out what he remembers and what he doesn't. Of all the things I'd think Finn would remember, it would be sex. Let's be honest here. He might forget his own name, but the location of the clitoris is another matter."

They turned back to Willow for the answer. "He…knew what he was doing," she explained delicately. She wasn't about to tell them that she wasn't experienced enough to know if his skills were unusual. All she knew was that it was the most incredible night she'd ever spent with a man. "He was a thoughtful and generous lover—" She stopped, certain she was blushing brighter than that red gown from earlier.

"Generous and thoughtful?" Kat scoffed. "That doesn't sound like the Finn I know. Certainly not the one that did this." She rubbed her belly thoughtfully.

"Honestly, I've yet to see the Finn we know," Jade added. "He looks like Finn and sounds like Finn. But it's more like an alien is wearing his skin."

Willow frowned. She'd heard several things from his family since they arrived that had given her pause about her relationship with Finn. He'd obviously been some kind of playboy. But other adjectives had been included in not so many words—selfish, irresponsible and a bit of a jerk. Things were okay between them for the moment, but what if Finn's memory came back? What if he returned to being the arrogant womanizer he once was? It would be over between them for sure. There was no way a man with Ferrari tastes in cars and women would be interested in the stripped, broken-down hatchback that was Willow. Not even a fancy paint job courtesy of his sisters could help her if the old Finn came back.

"Maybe his memory won't come back," Jade offered as though she could read Willow's mind. "Then he could just stay the polite, kind Finn we know now, and we'd get to keep you."

Willow perked up. "Keep me?"

"Yeah. We aren't sure when Tom will settle down, but we were pretty certain Finn was a confirmed bachelor. But the new Finn really seems to like you, Willow. Like Morgan said, he's never acted the way he does with you around any other women before. If the new Finn stayed around, you could get married and you'd be one of us."

Apparently she wasn't the only one inclined to flights of fantasy. "That's—um…that's not going to happen. Even if the new Finn stays around forever, I have a life on the other side of the country. I'd be crazy to give that all up for a man I've known less than a week."

"You can write your books anywhere," Jade pointed out.

"And Finn isn't just any man. He's one of the Steele heirs. Most women would do a hell of a lot more than move cross-country for them," Morgan said.

Willow sighed. She would intentionally lose this

argument because she couldn't tell them the truth. The truth was that Finn didn't know all of her secrets. He didn't know that she had been sick. Or that she could never have his children. As close as they'd gotten, they'd only known each other a handful of days. "I wouldn't get too attached" was all she said. "To the new Finn or to me. We will probably both be gone by the end of the week."

Jade frowned and turned back to the display of dresses. "Well, in that case, we at least need to make sure you look so amazing, he never forgets you. What about this one? Even I look like I've got curves in this cut."

She held up a peacock blue, empire-waist gown. It had wide satin straps, cap sleeves, a square neckline and a flowing chiffon skirt. It might be just the style she needed to disguise her lanky, waifish figure and less-than-stylish mastectomy bra.

"That color would be gorgeous on you."

"I love it," Willow said. "But I don't have anything to go with that color. I'd need shoes at least. Maybe some earrings so I don't look so plain."

"That is not a problem," Jade said. "We're nowhere near finished with you. We'll hit the makeup area, the jewelry counter, the shoe department… You'll walk out of here looking like a million bucks."

Willow wouldn't be surprised if it cost that much, too. She tried not to even glance at the price on the dress Jade chose. It would just make her anxious.

She had to tell herself it was an investment piece. Maybe one day she'd win a book award like the Agatha and need a gown to wear to the ceremony.

"Absolutely," Kat agreed. "Try it on and if you love it, we'll get the rest after lunch. I'm starving."

"You're seven months pregnant. You're always starving," Morgan pointed out and glanced down at the time on her phone. "It's just now eleven. We'll get you some pretzel bites a few shops down to tide you over."

"That's not true," Kat grumbled and followed the others into the dressing room. "But I want a frozen Coke, too."

Everyone was looking at him. It made Finn uncomfortable. He might've been the life of the party at one time, but at the moment he wanted nothing more than to be sitting on Willow's deck, scratching Shadow behind the ears and listening to the birds in the forest that surrounded them.

What gave him the most discomfort was the way the women were looking at him. There had been coy smiles, winks, blown kisses and overly grabby hugs from women who varied from barely legal to his mother's age.

He was desperate for Willow to come downstairs and join the party. He wanted her on his arm tonight. Not just to deflect attention from the female party guests, although that would be nice, but because he missed her. He'd gotten used to having her around all the time. It physically pained him when she was gone, like a piece of him was missing. He was certain this was a new experience for him, although he wasn't entirely sure he liked it. He was an independent guy, from all reports. But if that meant Willow wasn't in his life, then forget it. Nothing said he had to stay the same person forever.

He looked anxiously at his watch and then scanned the ballroom for the tenth time. It was filled with people dressed in their finest sipping champagne and nibbling on canapés. There was an orchestra playing on the stage and a dance floor with a few couples taking a spin. It was very nice, but difficult for him to believe tonight was all in his honor.

That's when Finn saw her.

At least he thought it was her. The woman who found him on the beach had changed from an island hermit to his fantasy come to life. She wore a dark teal dress that flowed around her legs when she walked, as if she were some kind of goddess. Gold-and-aquamarine peacock feathers dangled from her ears, and a headband of tiny golden flowers was nestled into her short blond hair. When her eyes met his from the other side of the ballroom, she smiled brightly and the look was complete. The hair, the makeup… It was perfection.

But it wasn't the fancy clothes and jewelry that made the difference. Willow was already a diamond.

His sisters had just given her the confidence that allowed her to shine.

When she looked at him like that, the crowd around them faded away. He turned abruptly from the stranger making small talk and made a beeline straight to Willow. He stopped long enough to pluck two flutes of champagne from a nearby server and held one out to her when he approached.

She accepted the drink and took a large sip. "So," she said with a nervous quaver in her voice, "do I look okay? If I don't, I'll go. I know that this isn't really where I belong and I don't want to embarrass you in front of your family and friends."

"Are you serious?" he asked. "You're the most beautiful woman at this party."

Willow glanced around the room at the other guests and then frowned at his champagne glass. "How many of those have you had tonight?"

"I am not drunk. You look amazing and I won't hear another word on the subject."

Finn spied his mother coming his direction with some stranger in tow—another person she wanted him to meet that he wouldn't remember. Reaching out for Willow's hand, he asked "Do you dance?" as he pulled her toward the dance floor.

If her answer was no, it was too late. It was his only viable escape and there were worse ways to go about it than pressing a beautiful woman's body against his own.

He wrapped his arm around Willow's waist and guided her with him in slow motion in time to the music. Leading her even in the simplest steps was a struggle as she fought his every move. She was stiff as a board and probably none too pleased with his abducting her onto the dance floor.

"I'm sorry," he leaned down and whispered into her ear. "I can't take any more of these conversations. It's been one stranger after the other asking the same stupid questions about my amnesia and if I really don't remember the accident. Or feeling me up."

Willow tilted her head up to look at him with an arched eyebrow of confusion. "Feeling you up?"

Finn sighed and nodded. "I get the feeling half the women at this party have spent the night with me, or would like to. It's incredibly disturbing."

Willow looked around the crowd of people and back at Finn. "If that's true, you have good taste. I've never seen so many beautiful women in one room before. They're probably all asking themselves why you're dancing with me."

"What does that mean? Why wouldn't I dance with you?"

"Because—" she frowned and averted her gaze "—it only takes a quick glance to see you could do better."

Finn groaned. "I thought we agreed this discussion was over and you're gorgeous."

He couldn't tell if Willow rolled her eyes, but

he imagined that she did. To prove his point, Finn leaned his hips against her own, pressing the heat of his arousal into the soft curve of her belly.

She looked back at him with wide eyes that eventually faded into a smirk. "Fair enough. Your sisters did an amazing job on my hair and makeup. And they helped me pick a stunning dress for tonight. I will give them full credit for the transformation. Maybe you're right and I look just as glamorous as every other woman here tonight. But even then, I'm uncomfortable. These people...they're all looking at me. They know I don't belong here."

"They're all looking at you because you're beautiful and they're jealous." He ignored Willow's scoff. "Apparently it's not every day that a woman catches and keeps the attention of Finn Steele. Or so I hear. But don't feel bad. I'm uncomfortable, too. Maybe more uncomfortable than I've ever been. I know my memories don't go back very far, but I'd take another round of broken ribs spent in your recliner over being at this party another couple of hours. It's unbearably awkward knowing they all expect something from me that I don't know if I can deliver. But you know what?"

"What?"

"This party is for me. And if I have to stay, I'm going to enjoy myself."

Finn dipped his head down and captured Willow's peach-painted lips with his own. She melted into his arms at last. Here, now, with her mouth open to him and her anxieties gone for a fleeting moment, he savored it. The party, the people, the awkwardness…they were all worth it because they brought Willow into his arms like this. While they'd come together physically, they'd never really had the opportunity for romance. He hadn't known until recently that he had the money to take her out to a secluded dinner for two or a nice supper club with dancing. They'd never dressed up and gone out on the town. But they had tonight and he wanted to make the most of it.

The song ended and with it, the spell he'd managed to cast around them. The world returned, and Finn noticed his older brother, Tom, joining the orchestra on stage.

"Ladies and gentlemen, if I could have your attention for just a moment, please."

A quiet fell across the room with everyone turning to the stage. Finn and Willow turned, as well, although he did it with more dread than interest. He wasn't aware there were going to be any speeches tonight. Hopefully they didn't expect him to make one. Just the thought of being up there with the spotlight on him made his palms start to sweat.

"For those of you that don't know me, I'm Tom, the oldest of the Steele children. We're here tonight to celebrate the miraculous survival of my younger brother Finn."

He paused long enough for the crowd to cheer. "But I wasn't surprised when I got the call that he was okay and coming home. You can always count on Finn to get out of a tough spot unscathed. I remember his freshman year in college, when he got caught literally with his pants down with the daughter of the dean of the university. You or I would've been expelled, but somehow, Finn became a campus hero and got into the most badass fraternity on campus without having to pledge."

Tom paused for more laughter. "And then there was the incident with the ambassador's wife. Dad paid dearly to keep that out of the news. And the time he seduced three Victoria's Secret angels over the course of New York Fashion Week alone." He shook his head. "You can't make this stuff up. Right now Finn doesn't remember any of it, but I'm sure a lot of us will never forget. I'm also certain every father in China breathed a sigh of relief when he left Beijing and their daughters behind. He was and is a legend. To my brother Finn!"

The crowd raised their glasses and cheered with laughter and appreciation at Tom's stories. A few people slapped him on the shoulder in congratulations for his notorious exploits. But Finn felt nothing but embarrassment. Embarrassment and a sudden, overwhelming sense of panic.

Finn gripped the stem of his champagne glass

so tightly, he was surprised it didn't shatter in his hand. But it didn't matter. In that moment, the flood of memories was all he could focus on. With imperfect timing, the dam of Finn's amnesia gave way and he remembered it all in a rush. Now he knew his brother wasn't exaggerating. In fact, he'd left out quite a few of the salacious details to avoid scandalizing Grandma Ingrid and Mother.

Up until this moment, he had thought that perhaps his reputation had been embellished. Perhaps it was just the family joke to pick on him for refusing to settle down. But it wasn't a joke at all. It was fact.

So many women. It made his stomach ache thinking of how casually he had used them all. Even Kat. He disgusted himself with the memories he could no longer ignore.

"Are you okay?" Willow leaned in and spoke into his ear over the sounds of the people talking on stage.

"I need to get out of here," Finn said. Reaching for her hand, he dumped his champagne glass onto a nearby table and fled for the door.

"What's wrong?" she asked as they made it outside.

"Be right back with your car, Mr. Steele," the valet waiting out front said, and jogged into the parking lot.

Finn bent over and braced his hands on his knees,

drawing in a cool breath. "I think I'm having a panic attack."

"We should go back inside. You can lie down upstairs."

"No!" he said more brusquely than he intended to. "I want to go home. I don't want to be around these people or in this house for a second longer than I have to."

"What happened?" Willow asked. "What set it off? Your brother's speech?"

Finn shook his head. He wouldn't tell her the truth. He couldn't. It was bad enough that he had to remember his past and come to terms with what he had done and who he had been. He didn't like himself. And he was afraid that Willow wouldn't like him, either. Not if she knew the truth. If he was honest with her about what he'd done and how he'd treated the people in his life, she would never want to speak to him again. And he couldn't bear the thought of that.

Willow was the only thing in his crazy life that made any sense. She was the anchor that kept him from being swept away by the currents. He wasn't about to drive her away any sooner than he had to.

The valet returned with his Ferrari. He tipped the driver and they got inside. Moments later, they were peeling out of the long driveway and onto the highway, getting far, far away from the Steele mansion and the memories it held.

But running away from his family only did so much. His past had returned and no matter what he said or did, it would follow him forever.

Nine

Everything was different now.

Last night, as they'd entered his town house for the first time, it had been like touring an old historic house. He'd expected to see placards explaining the different pieces of art and furniture. There was no connection, even as he looked at his own face smiling back at him from pictures.

Now, with Finn's memory suddenly restored, it was more like a haunted house than a museum. Everywhere he looked, he saw ghosts of the past. Female ghosts, mostly. And unlike at the party, he couldn't run away from his own history.

With a sigh of relief, Willow kicked out of her

heels. "I looked good while it lasted." She made quick work removing her jewelry and massaging her abused earlobes.

"Yes, you did. I'm sure everyone will think I swept you out of the party early to make love to you." And that was true enough. He'd done it on multiple occasions over the years when he'd been forced to attend one of the company's tedious fundraisers.

"Is that why we left?" Willow asked. She turned her back to him and presented the zipper to her gown. "Please."

Finn moved instinctively to her back. Ignoring the zipper at first, he opted instead to run his palms over her bare upper arms, warming her skin. He leaned in to press a firm kiss against her neck, appreciating the accessibility her short haircut provided. He loved a woman's neck and the reactions he could coax by caressing it. He could feel her shiver against his lips and smiled.

Running his fingers across her shoulders, he traced the line of her back down to her zipper. He tugged it down slowly, grazing the silk camisole he found beneath it as he traveled to the low curve of her spine. He bit his lip to smother his disappointment. He'd been hoping somehow that tonight of all nights, she might be bare beneath that gown. He still hadn't managed to convince her to take off her top.

"Maybe that is why we left early," he whispered

into her ear. "Maybe I faked that panic attack just to get you into my bed."

Willow turned in his arms to face him, holding her dress to her chest. "Liar." With that word hanging between them, she turned and headed for the staircase.

"You don't think I want to make love to you?" he asked as he followed her upstairs and into the master suite.

"Oh, I believe you want me. I just don't think that's why we left early." She punctuated her sentence by letting the gown slip to the floor.

If she had to be wearing something beneath her gown, Finn had to admit this wasn't so bad. The ivory silk chemise was edged with scalloped lace that fell high on her thighs and dipped low at the neckline. She was wearing a bra beneath it, as usual, but it was more skin than he'd seen on her chest so far. Admiring the view, he halted when he noticed an unusual scar beneath her collarbone. It seemed like a fairly new scar, making him wonder what else she might be hiding with her modesty.

Willow paid him no mind as he studied her, focusing instead on scooping up her gown and draping it over the nearby chaise lounge. She slipped her headband off and set it on the dresser with her earrings. Finally, she turned back to face him. "So are you just going to stare at me, or are you going

to tell me why we ran out of that party like your ass
was on fire?"

Finn looked at her for a moment, weighing his
options. He didn't want to lie to her, but he couldn't
tell her the truth. Not yet. She'd come cross-country
to help him with his transition home. If she knew he
had his memory back, she might not have a reason
to stay. Especially knowing what Finn was really
like. He knew he would have to tell her eventually,
but not tonight. Things would fall apart soon enough
when she figured out how unlovable he really was.

"It was my brother's speech," he said, which was
true enough. He sat down on the edge of his bed
and tugged at his bow tie. Lying to Willow made
his throat tighten and he thought it might help to
loosen his tie. It didn't. "Everyone seems to get a big
laugh from my old escapades. At my expense. But
I don't think any of it is very funny. It's one thing
to go through what I have and lose my memory. It's
another completely to not understand or even like
who I used to be."

Willow's expression softened as she listened to
him speak. She crossed the room and sat down on
the bed beside him, putting a comforting hand on
his knee. "You don't have to have amnesia to not like
who you are or to feel uncomfortable in your own
skin. I think a lot of people do, but are too scared to
change or don't know how."

Finn shook his head. "But what if I can't change?

What if my memory returns and I end up falling back into my old habits again?"

"Finn, if you want to change, you can at any time, memory or no. You're already so different from the man I've heard people describe. Being a womanizer or not is completely within your control. It's not like you have an awful medical condition or were in some disfiguring accident that can't be helped or changed."

There was something about the way she said the words that made Finn take notice. It made him wonder if she was speaking from personal experience. "Like you?" he asked, turning to look at her.

Willow opened her mouth, then closed it again. She turned away from him and focused her eyes onto the floor. "Yes," she said at last.

He put his hand over her own. "Tell me, Willow. Please."

She sat for a moment before she spoke, making Finn's stomach knot tighter with every second that ticked by in silence. "I told you about my mother. And my grandmother. We found out too late that they were both at a higher risk of developing cancer because they had the BRCA gene that increases their odds of getting both breast and ovarian cancers in their lifetimes. After they both got sick, my sister and I were tested and we had the gene, as well. Having the gene is not a guarantee, but with the family history, I knew it was only a matter of time.

Two years ago, I found a lump and I knew what it meant for me.

"After watching what happened to my mother," she continued, "I decided that I wasn't going to mess around. My sister said I was being paranoid, but I didn't care. I was determined to live past forty-five and not pass on this curse to anyone else. So I had a complete mastectomy and hysterectomy. Then I underwent months of chemotherapy. I lost thirty pounds and what curves I had were long gone. So much of my long blond hair fell out that I had to shave my head. This scar—" she touched the area of her chest he'd noticed earlier "—is from where they put my chemo port."

Finn squeezed his eyes shut. He'd been blind to not see how all the puzzle pieces of her life fit together to create this terrible image. Blind or just selfish—he'd been focused too much on his own problems to see she'd obviously been through a lot. She was living basically as a hermit, hiding from the world for a reason. Her short haircut and small figure. The panic attack in the hospital when she saw the cancer patient. The fact that she refused to take off her shirt for him… Separately those things didn't mean anything, but all together, the answer was obvious.

"Why wouldn't you tell me about any of this?"

Willow sighed. "It's not easy to talk about, Finn. I'm no spokesperson for breast self-exams. And it's not necessarily something I feel the need to tell a stranger that drops into my life out of nowhere."

"Is that how you still think of me? After everything we've gone through this week? After all the things we've shared? Even after we made love?"

"Of course not," Willow said. "But by the time I felt comfortable enough to tell you about my past, I didn't *want* to tell you."

He didn't understand. "Why?"

"Because on some level, it's embarrassing. I'm damaged goods, Finn. Who would want me if they knew the truth?" She turned to look at him with tears shimmering in her eyes. "For one thing, I can't have children. And for another, I didn't have the reconstructive surgery. I couldn't bear to face another painful procedure when it wasn't medically necessary. I was tired of needles and drainage tubes, medication and discomfort. I wanted it to be done. Under this chemise…" Her voice trailed off.

Willow shook her head. "I don't want you to see. I didn't want anyone to ever see. So I hid away from the world to protect myself."

Finn listened to her speak without interruption. He could feel the weight of her words as she confessed her truth to him. He'd arrived in her life and disturbed the peace she'd tried to build herself. He'd tempted her from solitude and forced her, without knowing it, to face her biggest worries and fears.

"And now, after seeing the life you've lived and

the women you've known…how could I ever compete with them? They're a bunch of gorgeous lingerie models and I'm…well, not. So I'm sorry if I don't seem to believe you when you tell me over and over that I'm pretty, Finn. It's because I know the truth. I've seen the ugliness that I've kept hidden from you."

Once she'd gotten all the words out into the world, Willow could only hold her breath and wait for everything to come crashing down around her. Even if he'd cared for her, even if Finn harbored unspoken feelings for Willow…it might not be enough to overcome this. She'd told him all there was to tell. Short of taking off her top and exposing him to the harsh visual realities of her illness, it was done.

Now it was his chance to bow out gracefully, thank her for her help and let her return to the Pacific Northwest without making a bigger fool of herself than she already had.

"You're amazing," he said at last.

Well, that wasn't what she expected to hear. She turned to him and frowned. "Were you listening to me at all, Finn?"

"Yes, I was listening." Finn got up from the bed and knelt in front of her with his hands on her bare knees. Looking up into her eyes, he said, "And what I heard was the heartbreaking story of a tragedy that befell one of the strongest women I've ever met.

What I heard was the story of you fighting to live... of you making the hard decisions to keep from repeating the same fatal mistakes your mother made. You've lost so much and yet you still have so much left to give. I know because I've been the lucky recipient of your gifts."

Willow's mouth fell open. This was the point where he was supposed to tell her how sorry he was about her lot in life and walk away. And yet here he was, on his knees, telling her how amazing she was. She didn't know what to think or say to that, especially when she didn't believe it herself.

"I know it was difficult to share that with me. If I had lived a life like you have, I might be afraid to open up to another person. Thank you for sharing your story with me, Willow. I'm honored, and not entirely sure I deserve it, but I'm thankful you chose me."

"You're too hard on yourself," she managed to respond.

"I was about to say the same thing to you," Finn replied. "Maybe we're both right. But you rehashed your painful past tonight because you wanted to prove a point to me. You wanted to convince me that I could change and be a better man if I wanted to be. And you're right about that, too. You've gone out of your way to help me since the day we met. And now it's my turn to embrace the new, improved Finn Steele and help you."

"Help me?" Willow questioned. "What could you possibly do to help me? The damage is done."

"I want you to show me," he said.

Willow's heart sunk into her stomach. "No." Why would he ask such a thing of her? She didn't even like to look upon the scars herself. She wore a sports bra or tank top under almost everything, only showering without her scars covered up.

He took her hands in his and held them tightly. Probably so she couldn't escape the uncomfortable situation. "You've trusted me with your story, Willow. Now trust me with this. Please."

Finn was so stubborn. He wanted so badly to be different than he'd been in the past that he thought this was how he could do it. But he didn't understand that if he was repelled...if he even flinched at the sight of her chest, it might not help him at all, but it could set her back months, even back to square one on her mental recovery from her cancer.

"I want to make love to you tonight, Willow. But I want to make love to all of you. I want to touch and kiss every inch of your body. I don't want you to hide anything from me anymore. You're just one step away from being completely open and you need this. You've been so brave through the whole ordeal. Be brave now. I promise that this step may seem hard, but you've been through so much worse."

Willow looked down at him. He was so sincere in his words. And maybe, just maybe, this wouldn't be the nightmare she'd imagined it to be. In reality, there wasn't much risk in trying. With the party over and Finn settling into his old life, she would return home soon anyway. Either he accepted how she looked, or he didn't, but either way, she would be gone before long. Why not take the chance?

Deep down, Willow knew that was a lie. There was a risk. A huge risk. But it had nothing to do with her pride. It had to do with her heart. She had let herself fall in love with Finn. It was stupid, but she had done it anyway. If she wasn't in love with him, she never could've told him the truth about her past and she wouldn't even consider exposing her scars to him. Whether their relationship ended with a whimper or a bang, it would end and she would be crushed. But that ship had already sailed with her heart aboard. She might as well enjoy the cruise.

Without speaking, Willow untangled her hands from his and reached up for the silk straps of her chemise. She let them fall down her arms and slipped out of them until the cool fabric pooled around her waist. Then she reached behind her to unfasten her mastectomy bra. She closed her eyes, held her breath and let it slip to the floor. Then…a long and incredibly painful silence.

His hands were still on her knees, so she knew at least that he hadn't recoiled from her. But he hadn't said anything, either, which was unlike Finn. Finally, the curiosity got the best of her and she opened her eyes.

Finn was kneeling before her, just as he had been. He was looking her in the eyes with a soft smile curling his lips.

"Did you even look?" she asked. Was he playing the good guy by keeping eye contact and just not looking so he couldn't make a mistake?

He nodded. "Yes, I looked. I imagine that was incredibly painful to go through. But it isn't the most interesting part of you, by far, and I wanted to look back at your lovely face. I think I like looking at it the best. I can see all your emotions dancing there without you saying a word."

Willow looked down at her own chest for a moment and then back at Finn. If it didn't bother him, maybe she could work toward not letting it bother her anymore, either. Perhaps she'd built this all up in her mind to be worse than it was. Or maybe Finn was just deserving of the love she wanted to give him.

"I don't want you to ever be ashamed of your scars, Willow. Especially not around me. They're proof that you're stronger than the cancer. They're evidence that you're still alive. Be proud of them."

She didn't feel proud. She always felt like her actions were ones of fear, not strength, but she'd never wondered how it appeared from the outside looking in.

"May I?" he asked, reaching out to touch her.

She nodded, closing her eyes again. A moment later, she felt his gentle caress brush over her collarbones, her sternum and then lightly over her scars. It was a strange sensation. Some parts of her were numb, while others were very sensitive, but she didn't mind this. He seemed to intuitively know how to touch her. This felt right, where little else had in ages. It even managed to set alight the flame of desire for him deep in her belly.

Opening her eyes, she covered his hand with her own, then leaned in to kiss him. "Make love to me," she murmured against his lips.

Still on his knees, Finn slipped out of his tuxedo jacket and tugged off his bow tie. With a sly smile he sought out the hem of her chemise and pushed it up her thighs until the entire thing was a silk band encircling her waist. She watched as his fingers gently stroked her upper thighs, his hot breath searing her bare skin. She leaned back and braced her hands on the mattress when his fingertips grazed across the satin of her panties. Finn applied pressure to just the right spot and a bolt of pleasure shot through her.

"Oh, Finn," she whispered, her eyes fluttering closed. She felt his hands seek out the waist of her panties and gently start tugging at them, along with the bunched-up slip. Willow lifted her hips, and he slid both garments down the length of her legs to the floor. Now she was completely naked for the first time with Finn. For the first time with anyone since her surgeries.

Maybe that was why tonight felt different from the other times they'd come together. There was a newfound confidence in Finn's touch as he let his hands roam all over the soft skin of her bare thighs, creeping higher and higher. She worried for a moment that he was focusing below her waist and avoiding her chest, but then she felt the flutter of his touch as he brushed over her center and all thoughts faded away. An explosion of sensation took its place as one finger slipped inside and stroked her aching core. Her heart started racing in her chest as he pushed her closer and closer to her release faster than he ever had before.

Her orgasm was hard and intense, knocking her back onto her elbows with the powerful spasms. He stayed there on his knees until the last tremors shook her legs, and then he stood up.

He immediately had his hand at his collar, quickly unfastening the buttons of his shirt. He tossed aside his shirt and whipped off his belt. Willow sat up to help. Her fingers sought out his fly, undoing the button and pulling the zipper down. Her hand slipped inside, slowly stroking the firm heat of him through his briefs.

"Willow," he groaned, and then his mouth greeted hers. She met his intensity, stroking him with a sure, firm hand until he pushed forward and she fell backward onto the bed.

Before she could recover, Finn had slipped from his briefs and pants and was moving above her. The heat of his skin seared hers as he glided over her body. Willow's thighs parted, cradling him. He paused only as he met her gaze and hovered there.

He was such a beautiful man. The first day when she'd found him on the beach, she'd thought he looked like a fallen angel. The angles and curves of his face were perfectly carved by a great master. She had seen him at his worst that day, and at his best today. But her favorite expression was the one he had now as he paused, motionless over her. His golden hair had fallen into his eyes, his desire for her evident in his dark brown depths.

Was it possible that a man like this could ever love a woman like her? He was a successful businessman. A billionaire famous in the Charleston society circles. He'd probably grown up going to private schools and taking horseback riding lessons. What was Willow? A nobody born to a pair of hippies. Sure, she'd written some books and done well enough, but it felt like she could never do enough to deserve the love of a man like Finn, even though she wanted it so badly her heart nearly burst at the thought.

Finn dipped his head down to kiss her and she closed her eyes to focus on the sensation of being with him. She could feel the tears gathering in the corners as the unwelcome emotions of the night swelled inside her. Things between them had moved so fast, but she'd comforted herself in knowing they'd likely never go this far. She'd let herself indulge in a fling with her unexpected visitor figuring there wouldn't be any harm in it. But she was wrong.

His lips parted from hers, the air heavy and warm between them. Finn shifted against her, his spine arching and his hips moving forward. He entered her so slowly, and then paused there. Willow savored the sensation. She wanted Finn in her blood, his scent in her lungs, his taste on her lips, so she could keep him there in her forever.

His dark eyes searched her face for a moment as he hovered, buried deep and still inside her. "What am I going to do without you in my life?" he asked. "Isn't there a chance you might be willing to stay longer?"

Her secret hadn't driven him away. In fact, it had brought them closer. Was it stupid of her to run back to her island when she had something that felt special here? She needed to get as much of Finn as she could before it ended. "Maybe I could stay a few more days."

"Really?" A broad smile crossed his face.

"Yes, really."

Finn kissed her and the moment that had hung suspended in time suddenly began to rush forward.

Emboldened by her response, Finn eased back and thrust forward again. And then again.

Willow clung to him, riding the waves of pleasure as they surged through her body. She drew her knees up and locked her ankles together at the small of his back. She didn't want to let him go, not even for a second. This moment wouldn't last forever, but she would savor it as long as she could.

It wasn't long before Willow felt her release building up in her again. She bit her lip, trying hard to fight it off. It was too soon. "I'm not ready for this to end," she said. And she didn't just mean making love to Finn right this moment. She meant all of it. Adding a few days onto the trip was only delaying the inevitable. But he hadn't asked her to stay forever.

Finn propped himself up onto his elbows and planted kisses along her jawline to her lips. He kissed her thoroughly and smiled. "There will be more moments. Enjoy this one."

His hand slid up her outer thigh to her knee. He hooked her leg over his shoulder, tilting her pelvis up and driving harder and deeper than ever before. The sensation was incredible, causing Willow to cry out.

"Oh, Finn," she gasped, clawing at his back. There was no use in prolonging her release now. It was impossible. She could feel the tightening in her belly, the driving surge of the countdown inside her. "Yes!"

Willow sucked in a large lungful of air and her

eyes closed. Like a tsunami, her orgasm crashed through her. She clung to Finn for dear life as every nerve ending in her body lit up and her insides pulsated with pleasure.

"Willow…" he whispered, driving harder and faster than before until he stiffened and groaned. He gasped her name one last time as he surged into her body, leaving him exhausted and trembling.

He dropped over to her side, sucking ragged breaths into his lungs as his muscular chest rose and fell. They both lay together quietly for a few moments before Willow pushed herself up onto her elbow to look down at him. Damp blond curls were plastered to his forehead. His brow was furrowed from exertion as he lay there with his eyes closed.

"You're a better man than you give yourself credit for being, Finn," she said. "I don't think the old you would've handled this the way you did tonight."

He opened his eyes, looked at her and nodded with a sad certainty. "You're right. The old Finn was far too focused on the things that don't really matter. A woman's outsides aren't nearly as important as what's inside. A good heart, a sensitive spirit and a loving soul make for a far more beautiful lady than a big rack and pouty lips."

Finn rolled onto his side and reached out to caress her cheek. "And you, Willow Bates, are beautiful both inside and out."

Ten

Sawyer finally escaped the man who had been trying to talk business with him for the past hour. He scanned the mostly empty ballroom, looking for the wife who had long abandoned him to the boring chat. He found her sitting at a corner table, her shoes discarded and her bare, swollen feet elevated on a nearby chair.

"I'm sorry," he said as he approached her.

"This may have been the longest night of my life. If I was further along in this pregnancy I might've feigned labor just so we could leave."

"You know I can't leave these things early. Mother would notice."

Kat picked up her sparkling-water-and-fruit-juice cocktail and took a healthy sip. "And yet the guest of honor has been missing in action for two hours now."

Sawyer had noticed that he hadn't seen his brother or Willow in some time. A few people had even approached him, thinking he was Finn. "He usually finds an excuse to bail on these things early. Why did he leave?"

Kat shrugged. "The last time I saw Finn, the blood was draining from his face while Tom publicly humiliated him. I wouldn't be surprised if he escaped because of that."

Sawyer frowned at his wife. "Publicly humiliated? Finn? He loves telling those stories, especially because it gets my father all riled up."

"Maybe the old Finn enjoyed reliving his wild past. But the man that came home with you is different, honey. I don't think he's quite as proud of his escapades. He could barely look me in the eye since he got here. I don't know if he'll be able to handle being in the delivery room when Beatrice is born."

The orchestra finished their last song and thanked the remaining audience, signaling the end of the night. The catering team swarmed the ballroom, picking up the last of the dishware and breaking down the dessert bar.

Kat reached out her arms to Sawyer. "Take me home, darling. I'm through with all of this."

Sawyer knelt to slip her ballet flats onto her feet

and lifted her out of the chair. He wrapped his arms around her as best he could. "You know, we agreed this baby would never come between us," he said as he looked down at the gap her expanding belly created.

"Very funny," Kat said and gave him a quick, firm kiss. "I can actually feel myself getting bigger if I sit still long enough. The third trimester is not for wimps."

"That is the last word I would ever use to describe you. You hand-carved Beatrice's cradle. You're a force of nature." Sawyer wrapped his arm around her shoulder and walked her to the foyer. When their Range Rover was brought around, they settled in and headed back over the bridge to downtown.

"You know, I think I like the new Finn," Kat said after a few moments of silence.

"I do, too. And I like Willow. I feel like she's a good influence on him. I couldn't say that about any other woman I've seen him with before."

"The girls and I agree that she's a keeper. I hope Finn is on board with that plan."

Sawyer wasn't so sure about that. He'd never thought he would see the day when Finn settled down. Their father had twisted his arm into proposing to Kat when she got pregnant, but his heart wasn't in it. No one was more relieved when she turned him down than Finn was. "If Finn has

changed for good, you might get your way. But…"
He trailed off.

"But what?"

Sawyer frowned at the road ahead of him. "The doctors in Seattle said that Finn's memory would eventually return. They seemed to think it was a side effect of the swelling in his brain when he hit his head. It's not permanent. And when he does remember everything, I can't help but think things will change drastically. Especially between him and Willow."

"But he seems so disgusted by his old partying ways. You don't think that his experiences since the crash will affect him after his memory returns?"

He wished he could say yes for certain, but Finn always seemed to find a way to surprise him. "I don't know."

"Well, I'd like to think that even with his memories, Finn has changed for the better. He's had a near-death experience. And if you ask me, he's fallen in love with Willow."

"Finn?" Sawyer sputtered. "In love?"

"You've seen those two together. He may not want to admit it to himself or anyone else, but he loves her. If those two things combined don't make him want to seize the moment and make the most of whatever time he has with her, I don't know what would."

Sawyer turned their SUV onto Market Street. If

Finn really did love Willow, maybe Kat was right and the new Finn would outlast the amnesia. But the nervous ache in his gut told him it was a long shot.

"For everyone's sake, I hope you're right."

Finn crawled out of bed at dawn for possibly the first time in his life. He knew now that he was a night owl. If he saw this hour of morning, it was because he hadn't yet made it to bed. He knew a lot of things now. And that was why he couldn't sleep.

He'd watched Willow sleep for a while, looking peaceful and beautiful on the pillowcase. Of course, she'd slept like a baby. Not only had she been well loved, but she'd finally lifted a great weight off her shoulders. She slept the sleep of a happy, free conscience.

Finn poured hot water into his French press and silently cursed himself. He'd had his memory back for less than ten hours and he was already acting like the self-absorbed shit he'd always been. The same person he said he didn't want to be anymore. But he'd lied to Willow. She'd been by his side through this whole ordeal. She'd held his hand as he struggled with his memory and his place in the world. And when those memories finally came back, he kept it to himself and instead pushed Willow to be honest with him.

That was rich.

He pinched the bridge of his nose as he sat at his

kitchen island. Willow had given him everything he'd asked for last night. He'd pushed her to trust him because he knew she needed to let the hurt and shame go. But he'd never forgive himself for doing it while his own pants were aflame. He was the last person anyone should trust.

Finn needed to tell her he'd gotten his memory back. Sitting over his coffee, he considered half a dozen scenarios where he'd stage his memory returning in a dramatic fashion, and he realized he was only making the situation worse by piling on more lies. He just needed to be honest with her, no matter the cost.

And yet he knew what the cost would be. He had no doubt that he would lose Willow. Not because of the lies, necessarily, but because of the truth. If his memory had returned, Finn was no longer lost in a sea of strangers, fighting to understand a life that made no sense to him. She would go because he remembered now. He remembered everything. He knew why certain women had looked at him at the party with wicked, hungry gazes and why others seemed to scowl at him from the edges of the ballroom.

He wasn't lost. He didn't need Willow to hold his hand. At least, not like before. Now he was just confused on how to move forward with his life. If he didn't want to slip into his old bad habits, he had to make changes, as Willow had suggested. And he could. He was capable of being a better person. He could at least continue to be the person he'd become since the accident. But he got the feeling that the minute she returned to Washington State, those bad habits would resurface again.

Whether he was punishing himself for screwing things up with her, or just trying to forget Willow, he had no doubt he would party until her curious dark eyes stopped haunting him when he closed his eyes. And he knew that once he started down the path of booze and women, he wouldn't want to stop again. It was a hell of a lot more fun than being stuffy and responsible like Sawyer, or an ass-kisser like Tom.

Sure, finding out who he really was had carried the excitement of knowing he was rich and important. But there was also a peace and easiness in just being Jack, who didn't have a dime to his name but was happy with Willow in the middle of nowhere. Since Sawyer found him, it had been nothing but a roller coaster of emotions, culminating in last night's flood of unwanted memories. Being a Steele had baggage. And being Finn Steele made everything complicated.

"I woke up lonely in a cold bed."

Finn turned around to see Willow standing at the bottom of the stairs. She was wrapped up in a pink silk robe and wearing a pair of his bedroom slippers.

"I'm sorry," Finn replied, leaning in to give her a good-morning kiss. "I couldn't sleep."

Willow looked mildly surprised. "After all of last night's hard work, I would've thought you'd sleep like a baby."

"Well, you certainly slept like someone who had been thoroughly and well loved. Would you like some coffee?"

"Actually, if you have some, I think I'd like tea."

"I do. It's in the far-left cabinet above the canisters. There should be English breakfast and Earl Grey."

Willow was heading over to the cabinet when she stopped dead in her tracks and turned to look at him. "What did you say?"

That's when he realized what he'd done. Amnesiac Finn wouldn't know the first thing about what was in his cabinets or where, and yet the details had rolled off his tongue as easy as could be. He'd managed to blow it almost immediately.

"How would you know all that?" Willow pressed.

"I…" If anyone else had put Finn on the spot, he would've had a quick lie or comeback to deflect it. He could say he'd seen it earlier looking for coffee or sugar or anything. The lie hung on the edge of his tongue. But not with Willow. He knew what he had because he knew every inch of this home. "It's just tea, Willow," he said instead.

The expression of contentment she'd woken with started to crumple. She bit at her bottom lip and glared at him. "No, this is about more than the contents of your pantry, Finn. When we first got here, you couldn't even find the powder bath on this floor. How long?" she demanded. "How long have you had your memory back?"

He could see the overhead lights reflecting as a shimmer in her moist eyes. "A day? A week?" Willow's voice cracked as she spoke. "Has this whole thing been some kind of charade for you to get a break from your life and responsibilities for a while at my expense?"

"Absolutely not!" Finn insisted. Yes, he hadn't been completely honest with her, but to accuse him of lying about everything? That was a low blow, especially considering the shape he was in when he turned up on the beach. It was as though she'd been waiting for him to betray her this whole time. "I just got my memory back, Willow. I swear it."

"So you woke up with your memories this morning and decided not to wake me up and share the news?" She glared at him from across the kitchen island and dared him to lie again.

He sighed and looked down. "No, it wasn't this morning."

"Was it last night, then, at your big party? Did seeing all those beautiful women remind you of the nights you've spent with them? They were all certainly looking at you like they knew more than a casual stranger."

"It wasn't like that, either. It had nothing to do

with the women. They made me uncomfortable—I didn't lie about that. It was later, during Tom's awful toast. I don't know why that triggered my memories, of all things, but it did. That's why I wanted to leave so suddenly. It was too much for me all at once. All I wanted was to get away from all of those people who knew me before the accident and what I was like then."

Willow looked at him for a moment, studying his face carefully. Finn tried hard not to flinch under her scrutiny, or worse, to try and make himself look more honest and contrite. She would see right through that.

"I'm not sure I believe you, Finn. I'm not sure I believe anything you say now."

"No, please," he said, rushing closer to her, only to have her take a large step back. "It was last night. I was scared to tell you."

"So you decided to just lie? All the while, prompting me to trust you with my biggest, most painful secrets?" Willow looked down at the gap in the neckline of her robe, and tugged it tightly closed to keep her chest and everything that went with it hidden from his sight.

Fate had the worst timing. Why would his memory have to return on the same night she'd finally opened up to him? "No. Willow, don't associate last night with this. What we shared was so special to me."

"Everything that happened last night was tainted

by your lies. One of the only reasons I was comfortable sharing my scars with you was because I didn't think you could compare me to a hundred other women you've been with before. And the whole time, you had your memories of every single one."

"I assure you that the last thing on my mind last night was other women. Before and after my memory returned, you're the only woman I've thought about. How I feel about you. How special you are. How it would ruin everything if you knew the truth about me."

Finn shook his head. "I've been agonizing over what to do since before sunrise. The old Finn wasn't a very good guy. I thought once you knew my memories had come back and you learned what I was like before the accident, that you wouldn't want to stay. That's why I didn't want to tell you yet. I'm not ready to lose you, Willow."

She listened to everything he had to say and sadly shifted her gaze down to the hardwood floors. "I'm sorry, Finn, but you already have."

Willow had been dreading this moment since the amnesiac with the dimpled grin had captured her heart. She knew that when he regained his memories, she would lose him. At least, she would lose Jack. Jack was the man she had fallen for. Curious, kind, grateful…he had looked at her like his whole world was wrapped up with her on their tiny island.

He was an outsider when he showed up on her beach and they were able to be outsiders together. Jack would never lie to her. Or manipulate her. He didn't have a devious bone in his body.

But Finn was never hers. He was the billionaire heir of Steele Tools. The playboy. He'd never been an outsider. He'd always been the cool guy. Mr. Popular. She wouldn't even begin to know how to relate to a man like that. It was hard enough to make small talk with his friends and family. There was no way she could continue on with Finn when they had nothing in common but a week spent together on her island.

She would cherish the time they'd had together. It had been an enlightening and educational experience for her. Willow had realized by being with Finn that she might live on an island, but she wasn't one. Keeping people and relationships at arm's length might have seemed like the right thing to do after her health scare, but it only made her lonely. And worse—vulnerable to the charms of the first man who dropped into her life.

Even coming out here had taught her more about herself and what she was capable of when she put her mind to it. She had fought through cancer, making hard choices to ensure that she would live, and now she needed to start actually living. Despite what she once believed, she could still be beautiful and desirable and have people in her life. There were people out there, men included, who would accept her as she was, once she was able to do the same. But that man would not be Finn. Their relationship was a stretch, and it was time for the fantasy she'd built up in her head to end.

It was not what she'd intended to wake up to this morning. She'd hoped for a kiss, some caffeine and maybe a return to bed. Instead, she'd been faced with a truth she couldn't ignore any longer. It was so disappointing to watch him scramble for words when he was caught in his lie. She'd heard stories about his escapades, even masquerading around as his twin without anyone suspecting the truth.

She had thought that the infamous Finn Steele would be a better liar. And she wished he was better. Or that she couldn't read him so well. Then they could both keep on pretending that his memory hadn't returned. But he'd screwed up and there was no going back to the way things had been.

"Please, Willow. What can I do to convince you that I mean what I say? Tell me. I know that I shouldn't have lied to you, and I'll do anything to make things right between us again."

Willow bit at her lip, fighting to stay strong. This needed to end. And the sooner the better for both of them. "You are who you are, Finn. Nothing can change the past. And it seems like your future might be on the same path you've already set a course for. And that's okay. There's nothing wrong with continuing to live your life the way you'd planned to before the accident. You've just got to do it without me."

"Willow—" he started to speak, but she held up her hand to silence him.

"Please book me a flight back to Seattle as soon as possible," she continued. She wasn't going to wait to hear his arguments. If he had a good reason for her to stay, she might be persuaded to do it. And if she'd learned anything about the old Finn, it was that he knew how to get his way. She didn't believe the glint of tears or the pained expression on his face were intended to manipulate her, but she could feel her resolve crumbling from seeing him hurt. "I think it's past time for me to go home."

His dark eyes watched her with a mix of resignation and disappointment. She could tell then that he wouldn't fight her on this. He knew this needed to end, as well. They both needed to move on with their separate—and very different—lives. Their paths were never meant to cross. It was an accident. And now it was time to fix it and put their paths to rights.

"If that's what you want, I'll take care of all the arrangements. If you'd like to start packing, I'll have a car come pick you up and take you to the airport in about an hour."

"Thank you." Willow took a deep breath, resisting the urge to run into his arms and bury her face in his chest. Instead, she turned and went upstairs to pack her clothes and get ready to leave.

Her small duffel bag held what she'd brought with her, but she quickly realized there was no way that any of her new pieces from her shopping trip with the girls would fit inside. It was just as well. She would never have another occasion to wear a dress like that, despite what she'd tried to convince herself earlier. Maybe one of his sisters would like to have it. It would be lovely on Jade. She hung up the dress and put it in the closet with the heels. She opted to keep the earrings and the headband; they were easier to pack.

Dressed and ready, she checked the time. She had a bit before the car would arrive, but she couldn't just stay up here. She went downstairs, dropping her bag by the front door. She could hear Finn in the kitchen.

"Please tell the driver when he arrives that I'm across the street at Waterfront Park."

Finn walked into the room, drying his hands with a towel. "I will," he said with a nod. "He should be here in about fifteen minutes."

"Thank you." Willow reached for the doorknob.

"No. Thank you, Willow," Finn said in a quiet voice that reminded her more of her sweet Jack. "Thank you for everything."

She couldn't look at him. Not if she wanted to stay strong. "You're welcome," she replied and marched out the front door without looking back. She rushed across the street to the park and found a place to sit near the famous pineapple fountain.

There were people all around. Some were admiring the fountain, while others were looking out into the channel for the famous sights of Charleston Harbor. The whole area oozed Southern charm and history. Willow didn't see any of it. She was lost in her thoughts, lulled there by the roar of the fountain.

It wasn't until a man in a black suit tapped her on the shoulder that she returned to the world. "Miss Bates? I'm here to take you to the airport. I already have your bag in the car, along with all your flight information."

Willow followed the man to the street where the shiny black Lincoln Town Car was waiting for her. She was determined not to look over at Finn's town house as they pulled away. As she'd tried to tell Finn, there was no sense in looking back. Just look forward.

It was time to return to her solitary, but comfortable, life on Shaw Island.

Eleven

Monday morning, bright and early, Finn put on a suit and went to the Steele Tools corporate offices. He ignored the wary glances and whispers as he crossed the lobby to the elevators and headed to the executive floor. He supposed that surviving a plane crash made him subject to employee gossip. Among his other notable activities.

When he arrived at his office, his assistant, Melody May, shot bolt upright in her chair. "Mr. Steele?" she asked. "I wasn't expecting to see you this morning."

He admired the pretty, dark-haired woman who had worked as an assistant for the three Steele boys for at least the past two years. Finn had flirted with her, but to avoid more problems at work than he already had, he had maintained a hands-off policy with Melody. That seemed to offend her more than anything else. But today, she appeared to have put that chip on her shoulder in the past.

"You don't expect to see me most mornings, Melody." Finn smiled and walked past her desk to his office.

Melody showed up a few minutes later with a cup of coffee and a handful of cream cups and sugar packets. "I'm not sure how you take your coffee, sir."

Finn felt the burn of shame on his cheeks. He'd barely done anything to deserve this job and the salary it earned him. He couldn't even be troubled to show up before lunch most days, so much so that his own assistant didn't know how to make coffee for him. He really had been a jerk to everyone in his life. "Black, thank you."

Her brows rose slightly in surprise as she set the cup on his desk. "You're welcome, Mr. Steele. Is there anything else I can do?"

"Could you put a ticket in with IT to get me a new laptop and a new corporate phone? Mine were both lost in the crash. I also need all new identification cards, credit cards, a checkbook, a passport... and anything else I normally carried in my wallet. If you can help me work all that out, I'd very much appreciate it."

"Yes, sir."

"Please call me Finn."

"Yes, sir."

"Could you also print out my calendar for the next week so I have it to reference until my new computer shows up?"

"Absolutely."

"Thank you, Melody." The woman hesitated for a moment, making Finn feel even worse for how he may have treated her in the past. "Have I ever told you 'thank you' before, Melody?"

She sat with a puzzled expression on her face for a moment before shaking her head. "I don't believe so."

Finn sighed and sat back in his chair. "Well then, to the thank you, I'd also like to add that I'm sorry. Things will be different now."

"You really lost your memory, Mr. Steele?"

Finn nodded. No one but Willow knew it had returned yet. "Finn, please, Melody. But don't worry. These changes are permanent. The amnesia has nothing to do with my ability to treat people well."

Melody smiled and backed out of the room. "Let me know if you need anything else, Mr. St—*Finn*."

His assistant disappeared from the room, leaving him alone in the emptiness of his office. He looked around at the unremarkable space. The furniture was a generic mahogany suite with leather guest chairs and a small conference table near the window.

Both his brothers had similar setups. He'd added a small dry bar in the corner with a minifridge and a crystal decanter filled with Scotch. The bookshelves behind him were mostly empty, save for a few picture frames. He turned to look at them as though it were the first time.

Even with his memory back, it didn't seem very familiar. He'd never spent much time here and that had nothing to do with his assignment in Beijing. He was just a shitty employee who got away with murder because he was the boss's son.

One photo was of his whole family gathered for some event on the lawn of the estate. He couldn't remember which get-together it was for. Another was an autographed photo of him with an Italian runway model. The third was a photo of him from a ski trip in Switzerland. He didn't remember the name of the woman in the picture beside him. He wished he could blame that on the head injury, but he just frankly couldn't keep track of them all.

An unfamiliar beep sounded at Finn's desk phone. He pressed the blinking button beside the intercom label. "Yes?"

"Your father would like to see you in his office."

And that was why he rarely came into work.

With a groan, he picked up his coffee and pushed up from his chair. His father's office wasn't far, just in the corner of the building with the best views of downtown on both sides. It was positioned such that

Tom's, Sawyer's and Finn's offices were easily visible to him down the hallway, as were their comings and goings. Or no-shows, in Finn's case.

"Good morning," Trevor Steele said as his son appeared in the doorway of his office. "Come in."

Finn sat in the guest chair, where he got most of his tongue lashings, and settled in for his next one. Perhaps he was in trouble for leaving the party early on Saturday. Or for surviving the crash and somehow inconveniencing his father and the company in the process. Who knew? It was always something, though.

"I know you've been out of touch for a few weeks. And I'm not sure if you recall, but when your plane crashed, you were coming home from our new facility in Beijing. It was a big responsibility I gave you by sending you out there to set up our first manufacturing plant overseas. And I have to tell you that things are going very well. The project has been an amazing success and you had a major hand in that, Finn. I'm proud of you."

If Finn hadn't regained his memories, this conversation would've been nice, but it wouldn't have had the same impact. He tried not to visually react to his father's words, just smiled and nodded at the praise. But it was the first time his father had ever said those words to him. And he hadn't realized how badly he'd wanted to hear them until this exact moment.

"I understand that you've been through a lot, and

I don't want to rush you. But once you're fully recovered, I'd like you to take on more responsibility at the company."

At this, Finn's jaw dropped. He'd only been given the bare minimum to handle since he'd graduated from college. He got the feeling that his father only gave him the Beijing job to get him out of his hair for a few months. "Really?"

Trevor smiled at him and he almost didn't recognize that expression on his father's face. It wasn't his polite public smile, but a legitimate grin. "Really. I feel like this whole experience has changed you for the better, Finn. You've done a lot of growing up in the last few weeks and I'm hoping that this will be the start of great things for you and your involvement in the company."

"Thank you." It was all he could think to say.

"There's actually a few big projects coming up, so you can have your choice. When you're ready. Now, get out of here. Take a few more days. I don't want you rushing your recovery."

Trevor stood and came around the desk. He held out his arms and it took a moment for Finn to realize his father wanted a hug. He got up and hugged his father, accepting the paternal slap on the back.

"When I heard your plane crashed, it felt like a part of me died," Trevor whispered in Finn's ear. "I thought I'd never see you again and I had so many regrets. It looks like we both have a second chance. Welcome home, son."

"Thanks, Dad." Finn left the office and found himself standing stunned in the hallway.

Growing up as one of four children, Finn had been neither the oldest, the baby nor the cherished girl. He was one of the twins, not even a whole person on his own. He learned early on that getting into trouble got him more attention than being good. He also learned that it was a hell of a lot more fun. So he took on the mantle of problem child and made the most of it.

But deep down, if Finn was honest with himself, all he'd really wanted was for his parents to acknowledge him. Maybe even to be proud of him. But it had seemed impossible until now. The moment he'd always secretly wanted with his father had happened. And all it had taken was for him to nearly die.

He should be thrilled.

And yet…the moment wasn't everything he'd hoped for it to be. Or at least, it wasn't as impactful as he expected. To actually earn a promotion, more responsibility and the approval of his father…it was everything he'd dreamed of and suddenly nothing he wanted. And it was all because of Willow.

She could've gone through reconstruction to look the way the world expected her to, but she'd made the choice that was right for her. She lived a life that made her happy, even if her sister or outsiders thought it was strange to live alone. If he'd learned nothing else from his time with her, it was that he needed to live his life on his own terms. Despite his wild reputation for hedonistic fun, he hadn't really been happy. Or fulfilled. Everything he'd ever done had been to suit his chosen role as the rich playboy son. Living in the moment had been fine enough in his twenties. But now he wanted to do what made him happy and that meant rebelling in a completely different way.

Finn had thought chasing women and partying at every opportunity was a great way to spend his free time. Most people were envious of the life he lived. And that had been enough for him until he met Willow. Or rather, until he lost Willow.

Watching her walk out of his town house had been more painful than waking up on that beach a broken man. It was like she had ripped out a part of him and taken it with her. And he knew now it was his heart.

He had never been in love with a woman before, but he was pretty sure that's what it was. He couldn't stop thinking about her and what she was doing. He smiled remembering things she'd said to him. All of his public escapades seemed frivolous and stupid compared to a private life lived with her. She made him a better man, which was no easy task.

Everything about her was so amazing. And special. She wasn't just some cookie-cutter debutante. Willow was one of a kind. And he loved her.

Now he just had to find a way to prove to her that it wasn't too risky to love him back.

For the first time since Willow bought her house, it felt empty. Doc would be coming by later to bring Shadow home, but until then, it was just her and the rooms that seemed larger and more cavernous than she remembered. Big and abandoned.

It didn't help that the house had been left in a state of disarray. They'd basically gone to Seattle for the day to see the doctor and unexpectedly had never come back. She'd briefly returned to the house to pack some things for Charleston, but she hadn't had time to do much else. Finn's blanket was folded up in the recliner he'd loved to sit in. His empty coffee cup was still on the end table. Breakfast dishes were in the sink from that morning. Her notes from her latest book were scattered around her desk. It made it almost seem like Finn was still around. Like he would step out of the bedroom at any moment and ask her for some shampoo.

She had been alone in the house for far longer than she had ever been with Finn, but he had blended so seamlessly into her life, it was as though he'd always been around. People had always asked how she could live out here by herself, but it hadn't seemed to bother her. Maybe she just hadn't known what she was missing. But now, with Finn on the other side of the country, she truly felt alone here for the first time in her life.

Willow lowered herself into the recliner and gathered his blanket into her arms. Taking a deep breath in, she could smell Finn's scent lingering in the soft fabric. She could imagine burying her face in his neck and drawing in that same smell as she kissed his warm skin. Without much trouble, she could once again feel the stubble along his jaw as it grazed her throat.

Sitting back, she closed her eyes and tried not to let herself get upset again. She'd managed to hold her emotions in check until she was out of Finn's sight. She even made it onto the plane. But somewhere over Tennessee, Willow had started crying and couldn't stop until they were nearly to Salt Lake City. She always thought the people in first class lived such charmed lives. She was wrong.

At least about herself and her happiness. Willow had set herself up to fail in this situation. The moment she'd laid eyes on the beautiful, unconscious Finn, she knew she shouldn't get attached to him. She had a million different reasons, but the idea was the same—she needed to keep her distance or she would get hurt. She needed to protect herself and her heart. Without knowing the first thing about him, she knew that handsome face would never be hers.

To think otherwise was to court disaster.

And here, as she looked around her living room, was the disaster area. Ground zero. This was where she'd shared details of her life with Finn and he'd kissed her for the first time. Even as she'd pulled away from him, she'd known that a line had been crossed in her mind and her heart. A point of no return. Every moment she spent with Finn after that would only get her in deeper and deeper until she drowned.

And now she was all alone and hopelessly in love with a lying playboy she would never see again.

No. That wasn't exactly right. Truth be told, Willow was in love with Jack. The problems hadn't truly started until Jack morphed back into Finn. Until then, things between them had been simple and pure, somehow. Now their relationship was tainted by Finn's lies.

Willow was about to go into the kitchen and deal with the mess they'd left behind when she heard her house phone ring. She picked it up quickly, figuring it was Doc on his way over with the dog.

"Hello?"

"Where have you been, Willow? I've called the house almost every day for a week and no one has answered until now."

Willow frowned at her phone. It was her sister, Rain, who rarely if ever called, much less called repeatedly. "Is Joey okay?" she asked. The only reason she could think her sister might call that much was if there was an emergency with her young nephew.

"Joey is fine. We're all fine. You're the one I'm worried about."

"There's no reason to worry about me, Rain. I've been on a trip for a few days. Why didn't you call my cell phone? I had it with me the whole time."

Rain sighed into the receiver. "Willow, I don't know your cell phone number. Why should I bother when you never leave the house? I don't even know why you have one, to be honest. Do you get reception in the middle of nowhere?"

"I leave the house," Willow said, but it was a weak argument. Before Finn showed up in her life, she really only left the house to take walks with Shadow and to get food and supplies in Victoria. People rarely called on it, but the cell phone did work, despite her sister's concerns. "I've been in South Carolina for almost a week."

There was a long silence. "Why were you in South Carolina? Was there some mystery-book thing you forgot to tell me about? A book signing or something? I forget that you're a famous author sometimes."

"No, it wasn't for a book. It was a last-minute trip to Charleston. A vacation of sorts. I just got back into town last night pretty late."

"A vacation? By yourself?"

Willow's jaw tightened, holding in the words.

They weren't super close, but since she'd gotten sick, her older sister had attempted to take a motherly role. She knew that Rain wouldn't give up until she knew everything that was going on in her life. But that didn't mean she was going to spill about Finn at the first prompting. It was a long story with a painful ending and she wasn't sure she wanted to tell it yet.

"I was invited by a friend."

"Uh-huh."

"So how is Joey doing?" she asked in a weak attempt to change the subject.

"He's two. He's on the warpath destroying everything he can get his hands on. Steve wants to have another one, but I'm not sure I'm ready to start again. Now, who is this friend? Someone from the island?"

"Sort of."

"Sort of? Why are you being so difficult, Wil? What's going on that you don't want to tell me? Your cancer hasn't come back, has it? You did everything humanly possible to keep that from happening."

"No. No, my last scan was clear. I'm perfectly healthy." Just heartbroken.

She heard her sister audibly sigh in relief. "Then what is it? Something is going on, so tell me or I'll waste your whole afternoon. Or worse, I'll get on the ferry and come out there where you can't avoid me. You can't lie to my face, Willow. I can read you like a book."

"Fine, fine," Willow said, giving in. She really didn't want Rain showing up on her doorstep right now. "Did you read about the John Doe in the papers? The guy that just washed up out of nowhere with amnesia and no one knew who he was?"

Between the hospital's call to help identify Finn and Sawyer's attempts to find him, the story had made its way into the papers. She supposed it was just as well they had left Seattle before the reporters could swarm them with questions.

"I think Steve mentioned something about that. He pays more attention to the news than I do. What about him? Do you know him?"

"Well, yes and no. I didn't know him before his accident, but he actually washed up on my beach. Shadow found him when we were on a walk. Then we had that awful storm, so I was stuck taking care of him until we could get him to a hospital."

"I don't think I like the idea of some stranger at your house, Wil. Why didn't you say something?"

"What were you going to do? The ferries weren't running."

"Wait, I remember the story now. Didn't the papers say the guy had turned out to be some missing billionaire from that awful plane crash right before the storm?"

"That's the same man, yes. Once they figured out who he really was, I went with him back to his home in Charleston to make sure he got settled in okay. He didn't have his memory back and he needed some support. Then I came home. That's all there is to it."

"You went home with him. To the East Coast? That's not a quick trip. There's more to this than you're telling me."

"There is. And I'm sorry, Rain, but I just got back and I'm not really ready to talk about it yet. A lot of things have happened and I'm still working through it all."

"You love him."

How could she know? Her sister had a sixth sense about these things that had made Willow crazy growing up. "Yes, but it doesn't matter. It's over."

The slam of a car door outside caught her attention. "Listen, Rain, I've gotta go. Doc's pulling up outside with Shadow."

"Okay," her sister said with a dubious tone. "But this isn't over. We're going to talk more about this guy when you're ready."

"Whatever you say." Willow hung up the phone and got up from the recliner. Looking out the front window, she could see her enthusiastic dog leap from the cab of Doc's truck and run straight for the door with a loud *woo* of excitement.

Willow smiled and walked to the front door to greet him. She'd missed her fluffy boy these past few days. Maybe she'd let him sleep in the bed with her tonight.

She could use something to hold on to so she didn't feel so alone.

Twelve

It took two weeks for Finn to get his life in order. It was longer than he wanted, but upending his entire life would take a little time if he was going to do it properly. He started by gathering his family to make an announcement. He spoke quickly and firmly so they knew it wasn't up for debate. His memory had returned. He was resigning from Steele Tools and going to Washington State. Hopefully, to be with Willow, if she'd have him. But either way, he was done with his life as it was before the accident. No one protested. He hoped it was because they realized he'd finally found some direction in his life.

Next, he put his town house on the market and

the desirable property sold in a day. Then he sold the Ferrari. He donated most of his furniture and household things and packed what was important, which was surprisingly little. He took a few boxes to Sawyer and Kat's place and they agreed to ship them to him when he was ready. With a single suitcase, he boarded a commercial flight to Seattle and hoped for the best.

It was a bold step on Finn's part. He hadn't spoken to Willow since she walked out of his town house and flew home. But he knew that it would take bold steps to prove to her that he was serious. Serious about her and serious about the life he wanted them to start together.

He made a few stops in Seattle, the last being a boatyard near the coast. The salesman was stunned to have Finn walk onto his lot, point out a small but luxurious yacht model he'd had his eyes on for quite a while and hand him a check. The next morning, Finn and his new yacht were in the water and on the way to Shaw Island and his future.

Finn had always wanted his own boat. His parents had a large yacht—*License to Drill*—they took out for holidays and trips from time to time, and some of his best memories had been from those trips. Now that he was hoping to live on an island, it was the perfect time to buy one of his own, albeit much smaller. It would be practical, fun, and if he'd read her all wrong and Willow slammed the door in his face, he would at least have a place to live.

It was about ten in the morning when he rounded the shore near Willow's home where she had found him that first day. As he pulled up to her unused dock, he heard a familiar howling in the distance. He smiled. She and Shadow were on their walk.

Finn tied up the boat and stepped off onto the dock. His heart pounded loud in his chest as he walked across the worn boards to the grassy outcropping that separated the wooded area from the beach.

A moment later, Shadow leaped from the trees and made a beeline straight for him. Finn crouched down and welcomed the dog, who thankfully was happy to see him. Hopefully his mama would be, too. He accepted a few kisses and scratched the dog behind his ears as he vocalized excitedly.

"Shadow!"

The dog immediately turned and ran back to the trees, where he greeted Willow. She, however, barely took notice of the dog. Her eyes were glued on Finn. She was instantly stiff, as though she'd encountered a bear on her walk instead of the man she loved.

"Hello, Willow," he said.

The line between her eyebrows deepened as her gaze danced between him and the beautiful boat just behind him. "What are you doing here, Finn?"

He took a step closer to her, and she didn't move away. "I came to talk to you."

"You rich people are so dramatic. You fly cross-country and charter a yacht to come out here, when you could've just picked up a phone."

Finn shook his head. "What I needed to say couldn't be said over the phone. It needed to be done in person."

She narrowed her gaze suspiciously, but waited to hear what he had to say. "Say it, then. I've got a lot of work to do today."

She hadn't run excitedly into his arms and blanketed his face in kisses, but she hadn't slapped him and walked away, either. He took that as a positive. "I love you, Willow. There are a lot of other things I could say, but that is the most important one. You are the first and only woman I've ever loved. And not just because I don't remember. I remember everything, and nothing from my past has ever measured up to you."

Her lips parted in surprise for a moment, but she held her ground. "I know you think that you mean what you say, but I'm not so certain."

"You don't think I love you?"

"I think that returning to your old life and all your old memories was hard for you. Having to face who you've been and what you've done couldn't be easy. I imagine it's easier to run off to a faraway place and avoid reality for a little while longer."

"Is that what you think I'm doing?" Finn asked. "Running from my life?"

She shrugged. "You tell me."

"No. I'm running *to* my life, Willow. I realized that the life I had in Charleston was full of excitement and fun, but it meant nothing. I'd very nearly been wiped from the face of the earth in that plane crash and in the end, it hadn't really mattered if I lived or died. Sure, my family would be sad that I was killed, but it wouldn't change much, because I hadn't contributed much. I took and took, and I never gave anything back. And until you came into my life, I hadn't cared. But you made me want something more."

She watched him warily as he spoke. "When you were here before, you didn't know anything about your life. You were happy with soup and cereal, and walks in the woods. It's a simple life on this island. How do I know you won't get tired of slumming out here in the real world? That you won't decide to run back home and be a rich playboy again when things aren't going your way?"

"I don't have anything to run home to, Willow."

She crossed her arms over her chest and scoffed. "You have that big, beautiful house overlooking the harbor. That fancy sports car—"

"It's all gone," he interrupted. "I sold or gave away almost everything I had. The art, the furniture, all of it. But even if I hadn't, it was just stuff.

Once you left my house, it became glaringly obvious that it was just a big house full of things. The only memories that mattered were the ones I made with you, and it didn't mean anything without you there with me."

"You sold all your stuff, but you kept that cheap T-shirt and sweatpants I bought you?"

Finn looked down at the outfit he'd chosen to wear today. His San Juan Islands T-shirt and black sweatpants were perfect for a brisk day out on his boat. They were also a reminder of a happier time for him. "Of course I kept these. I kept everything that you bought for me."

Willow bit at her bottom lip. He could tell that her resolve was starting to wear thin. She wanted to believe him. She wanted to love him. He could see it. She was just scared to trust him. He'd hurt her and he couldn't expect the past to be wiped away as easily as it had before.

"So, you think you can just show up in that cheap T-shirt and say a lot of romantic things and I'll just forget about everything you did, right?"

"No. I don't expect you to forget. I know firsthand that forgetting just hides away the past—it doesn't deal with it. I only hope that in time, you can forgive. I'm not going to stand here and make excuses for why I lied to you. In the end, all I ended up doing was to drive you away when that was what I was trying so hard to avoid in the first place. But once you were gone, I realized it was far more serious than just wanting you there with me. I needed you with me. And not just to hold my hand through hard times. I need you because I love you, Willow. You took a part of me with you when you left that day, and no amount of money or women or alcohol would ever change that."

Willow swallowed hard and shook her head in disbelief. "You just gave up your whole life for me?"

"No," he said, pulling a small velvet box from the pocket of his sweatpants. "My life is here with you. And it always will be. All these years, I've been searching for something. I thought I would find it in the arms of a woman or in the approval of my father, but it never felt right once I got it. It turns out I had to forget about everything else to be able to see what I was looking for. I found it in you. You're my everything and I'm not going anywhere, Willow. Not without you."

Finn got down onto one knee in the grass and opened up the box to display the ring he'd chosen for her. "I love you just as you are, Willow Bates. And I hope that you can accept me as I am. I'm flawed. I'm complicated. But I love you so much, I couldn't stay away even knowing you might never want to speak to me again. I hope that you'll accept this ring and me along with it, to be my wife. There's nothing more in this life I want than to hear you say yes."

* * *

Willow had woken up this morning like she did most every morning. She anticipated a quiet day of writing and finally putting away the patio furniture since the season was long over. She was making a list for a trip to the mainland to get some new groceries. That was the highlight of her week. Or so she thought.

She had never expected to see Finn Steele again. And she certainly hadn't expected to be proposed to today. If she had, maybe she would've put on a nicer shirt or something. She looked down at the box Finn was holding out to her and couldn't believe the radical turn her day had taken. If she didn't know about his family and how much they were worth, she might think he was proposing with costume jewelry. It was that big and that shiny. Her mind was arguing with itself that there was no way the ring he was holding was real, but it had to be. The center stone was a bright yellow pear cut and easily six or seven carats. It was set in platinum with a thin split band that looked far too fragile to hold a stone that large.

"Is that—is that a yellow sapphire or something?" she asked. It was obviously not what he wanted to hear in response to his important question, but in the moment, she was so overwhelmed, she didn't know what to say.

Finn shook his head and stood up. He plucked the ring from the box and took her hand. He slipped it onto her finger, where it fit perfectly. It made her petite finger look even smaller with the giant stone. "It's referred to as a vivid canary diamond. They're very rare, especially in this size and quality. I actually had to buy the stone in an auction at Sotheby's in London, then I had someone from Harley's security agency fly over to England and escort it back to me. I had our family jeweler set it in a ring for you."

She couldn't stop staring at it. Partially because it was beautiful and partially because the significance of the moment had stolen the words from her lips. This couldn't be really happening. It looked like it should belong to Elizabeth Taylor or the Queen of England. Not on the hand of little, old, insignificant Willow Bates. "I don't know that I've ever seen a yellow diamond before."

"There aren't many, at least as many as bright in color or as internally flawless as yours. This stone is one in a million, easily. But so are you. You're my sunlight in the darkness. And I thought that there wasn't anything more ideal for you than a perfect bright yellow diamond."

"You certainly know how to apologize to a girl," Willow said as she fought the gathering of tears in her eyes. A yellow diamond was so perfect; he was right. And for reasons he didn't even know. It was like a drop of liquid sunshine on her hand. She hadn't thought Finn was that sentimental, but she was wrong. He'd obviously gone to a lot of trouble and expense to get this for her.

"I wanted you to know how sincere I was. I came out here with this ring and the boat, selling everything, so you would know I mean it when I say that I love you and I want to be with you. Whether or not you say yes, I had to come out here and try to make things right between us. I can't bear to think that you might hate me, even if you don't love me."

Willow shook her head and looked up at Finn. She couldn't let him self-flagellate any longer. "I could never hate you. I was hurt, but that was because I loved you so much. More than anything, I was angry with myself for falling for you when I knew that this relationship was destined to fail eventually. The odds were against us from the start, but I couldn't stop myself."

Finn visibly flinched at her words. "Do you still believe that? That we're destined to fail?"

"I think that the billionaire playboy and the reclusive mystery writer were never meant to be. But you and me, as we are now, I think we might have a chance."

"Does that mean you'll marry me?" he pressed.

Willow still hadn't given him an answer. She wanted to say yes. She wanted to scream it so loud that Doc could hear it from his property. But before she could, she had a question to ask Finn. "You said that you loved me just as I was, Finn. Did you really mean that?"

He clasped her hands in his and squeezed them tightly. "Of course I did."

"Even though we can never have a family of our own?"

Finn frowned at her. "Starting a family of my own is not something I've given much thought to. In fact, I've spent most of my life trying to prevent it. I never imagined that I would fall in love and want to get married. Until I met you. You're my family, Willow. And if it's just the two of us—"

Shadow nosed in between them at that moment and howled at being ignored for so long.

Finn gave him a pat on the head and a good scratch. "Pardon me, the three of us—then that's all the family I need."

"It doesn't bother you that I can't have your children? Please be honest with me because I don't want this to become something that comes between us later."

"If we wanted to add children to our lives, we could always adopt babies or foster as many of them as you'd like. Families take lots of different shapes and DNA isn't that important in the end. I love Morgan just as much now as I did when I thought she was my biological sister. And I love Jade even though she spent most of her life apart from us. That's not what's important.

"And even if it were," he continued, "I'm having my chance to have children. My daughter with Kat will be born before year's end. I don't know that I deserve to have the role of a father in her life, but I'd like to try. I'm already sharing her with my brother and Kat, and I think we'd all be happy to include you, too. Then she can have two dads and two moms that love and adore her. I think little Beatrice might be the luckiest girl in the whole world."

Willow had just been proposed to, and yet she'd never heard sweeter words than she had now. No matter what, she and Finn would be a family. And with his daughter, not only would she never have to feel like he was sacrificing his chance for children to be with her, but she would get a chance to be a mother. She'd never imagined that would happen for her. Or that any of this would happen for her. She took a big sigh of relief and looked up at him with a smile so big, it almost hurt. "I don't know about that," she said. "I think I might be the luckiest girl in the world."

Finn grinned and the elusive dimple in his cheek beckoned to her. She hoped that Beatrice would have that same dimple so she could kiss the baby's sweet cheeks just like her daddy's.

"That would make sense, because I'm the luckiest guy on the planet. Well, almost. Any other reasons why you think we shouldn't get married and be happy forever?" he asked.

Willow smiled and reached up to touch Finn's cheek with her hand, which was graced with a sparkling yellow diamond. "No. I think we've covered everything, so I'll put an end to the torture. I absolutely will marry you, Finn Steele."

With a loud whoop, Finn scooped Willow into his arms and lifted her off the ground to kiss her. She wrapped her arms around his neck and clung to him. Not just so she wouldn't fall, but because she never wanted to let him go. She'd done it once and she wasn't sure she could ever do it again.

Setting her back down on the ground, Finn looked at her with a wicked glint in his eye. "So, do you want to see our new boat?"

Willow grinned. "I absolutely do."

He took her by the hand and led her back down to the dock with Shadow jogging by their side. The closer she got, the more beautiful she realized it was. This was no boat. This was a fifty-foot Azimut yacht. The navy-and-white vessel tied to her dock was as sparkling and beautiful as the ring on her hand. She had always wanted something so she didn't have to depend on the ferry, but this was more than just a boat to get supplies. They could live on it. Travel the world on it.

He helped her on board and they climbed up to the sun terrace. "It can sleep eight, which is a little much, but it's the smallest one they make in this class. I could've custom ordered one, but I didn't want to wait any longer than I had to to cross the channel and get over here."

All she could do was shake her head. "It's beautiful. Perfect. Have you named her yet?"

"As a matter of fact, I have. They applied the name to the boat yesterday after I bought her. She's called *My Sunshine*."

Willow paused for a moment and looked at her new fiancé. Then she looked down at her ring. "What made you choose that?" He couldn't possibly know. Who would've told him?

Finn turned back to Willow and grinned. "I named my ship after my girl. That's a long-standing yachting tradition, isn't it, Sunshine?"

Willow's jaw dropped. "Who told you?"

"Well, after my sister mentioned that you wrote your books as S. W. Bates, I did a little digging."

"Oh, no," Willow said, squeezing her eyes shut.

"You knew everything about me almost as I learned about myself, but you…you were keeping secrets, love. When you said your parents were hippies, you didn't tell me everything. Rainbow Blossom and Sunshine Willow Bates," he announced with a smirk.

So he knew her full name. Her real name. "I haven't gone by Sunny since I left the commune. When we moved and I started public school, I told people to call me Willow. I just don't tell anyone because—" she looked at him and the amused expression on his face "—because of that!"

Finn scooped her into his arms and held her until she stopped squirming in irritation. "I promise it will be our little secret. And besides, your name will be changing soon anyway, Mrs. Steele."

"Willow Steele," she said, trying out the name. "I think I like it."

He tipped her chin up and captured her lips in a kiss. "I think I love it."

Epilogue

"Ho, ho, ho! Merry Christmas!" Finn shouted as he opened the front door of the Steele family mansion and stepped inside. He had a mountain of wrapped gifts in his arms and Willow by his side as they made their way into the foyer.

"We're back here, Finn dear," he heard his mother call out.

"Be prepared for the decorations to be over-the-top," he whispered to Willow as they walked through the main hall. Near the grand staircase was a small forest of trees with lights, silver-and-gold ornaments and a blanket of faux snow around their bases. Garland ran up each side of the staircase railing, and the scent of fresh pine and apple cider lingered throughout the house. "Mother loves Christmas."

"The tree-lined drive of twinkle lights and snowflake projections would've tipped me off even if the wreaths on each window and the garland wrapped around each column didn't."

Finn looked at his mother's handiwork with a new appreciation this year. He looked at everything with new eyes this year. His second chance at life had done that. As had Willow. And of course, his daughter. Christmas took on a whole new meaning with children in the house.

As they entered the family room, they were greeted by the twelve-foot-tall Christmas tree dripping in heirloom ornaments that sparkled in the light of the fireplace roaring nearby. As usual, the mantle was covered in garland and ribbons with stockings hanging there for everyone in the family. Thankfully, it was a large fireplace, as this year there were three new additions to the collection: one for Kat, one for Willow and one for tiny, three-day-old Beatrice.

Speaking of Beatrice, the Queen Bea was holding court in her grandmother's arms. Patricia was beaming as she held her granddaughter. Kat was resting in a nearby chair with her feet up and Sawyer hovering at her side in case she needed anything. The rest of the family was gathered around, looking at the new baby with grins on their faces and hot toddies in their hands. Beatrice, for her part, was un-impressed by it all and fast asleep.

Finn settled the presents with the others at the base of the tree. When he turned, Lena was waiting to offer them both a festive holiday beverage. "Merry Christmas, Lena," he said, leaning in to give her a hug. "You're looking radiant tonight, as always."

The woman's cheeks blushed bright red at his compliment. "You quit that, you old flirt. You're a father now, and soon to be a married man."

"I can still appreciate a lovely lady when I see one," he said with a wink.

He and Willow had settled into the couch together and he was just about to grab one of Lena's famous white chocolate–peppermint cookies when his father stood up.

"Now that everyone is here, I'd like to make a toast," Trevor said. Everyone quieted and held their glasses in anticipation. "This family has been through a lot the last few years. It's difficult sometimes to look back and think about those hard times, but then I always remember what amazing things have come from it. Without Jade being kidnapped, we never would've had Morgan in our lives. Or Jade's husband, Harley. We may have had our home bombed, but we came out of it with our new son-in-law, River, and the amazing charity in Dawn's memory.

"Finn brought Kat and our beautiful granddaugh-ter, Beatrice, into our lives. And now, in nearly losing him for good, we gained his lovely fiancée, Willow. In many ways, despite him living on the other side of the country now, we also got Finn back, too. I never could've imagined how our family would grow and change so quickly, and for that I'm grateful."

"Now if we can just marry off Tom!" Sawyer interjected from the corner.

Their oldest brother squirmed uncomfortably in the corner. "I'm working on it," he said. "I've been seeing a new girl lately and I'm pretty sure she might be the one. I knew the moment she was introduced to me at a party."

"What's her name?" Morgan asked.

"Becky. I thought that was appropriate."

Trevor laughed. "We've needed a Becky to complete my Mark Twain collection," he noted. "I look forward to meeting her. But in the meantime, to all of you, I wish you all a very Merry Christmas, and a happy, exciting New Year ahead."

"Cheers!" a few folks yelled out and glasses clinked together around the room.

Finn smiled and hugged his fiancée to his side. He knew that no matter what the future held for him, he would face it happily with Willow. He placed a kiss on the top of her head and raised his glass again.

"To Beatrice's first Christmas!"

* * * * *

#2821 HOW TO CATCH A BAD BOY
Texas Cattleman's Club: Heir Apparent • by Cat Schield
Private Investigator Lani Li must get up close and personal with her onetime lover, former playboy Asher Edmond, who's accused of embezzling—and insists he's innocent. With suspicions—and chemistry—building, can she get the job done without losing her heart a second time?

#2822 SECRETS OF A ONE NIGHT STAND
Billionaires of Boston • by Naima Simone
After one hot night with a handsome stranger, business executive Mycah Hill doesn't expect to see him again. Then she starts her new job and he's her *boss*, CEO Achilles Farrell. But keeping things professional is hard when she learns she's having his child...

#2823 BLIND DATE WITH THE SPARE HEIR
Locketts of Tuxedo Park • by Yahrah St. John
Elyse Robinson believes the powerful Lockett family swindled her father. And when her blind date is second son Dr. Julian Lockett, it's her chance to find the family's weaknesses—but it turns out Julian is *her* weakness. With sparks flying, will she choose love or loyalty?

#2824 THE FAKE ENGAGEMENT FAVOR
The Texas Tremaines • by Charlene Sands
When country music superstar Gage Tremaine's reputation is rocked by scandal, he needs a fake fiancée fast to win back fans. Family friend and former nemesis college professor Gianna Marino is perfect for the role—until their very real chemistry becomes impossible to ignore...

#2825 WAYS TO TEMPT THE BOSS
Brooklyn Nights • by Joanne Rock
CEO Lucas Deschamps needs to protect his family's cosmetics business by weeding out a corporate spy, and he suspects new employee Blair Wescott. He's determined to find the truth by getting closer to her—but the heat between them may be a temptation he can't resist...

#2826 BEST LAID WEDDING PLANS
Moonlight Ridge • by Karen Booth
Resort wedding planner Autumn Kincaid is a hopeless romantic even after being left at the altar. Grey Holloway is Mr. Grump and a new partner in the resort. Now that he's keeping an eye on her, sparks ignite, but will their differences derail everything?

HDCNM0821